NINE CHIMES

AUBREY KUBIAK

DEDICATIONS

To all the math lovers out there. May you always follow your heart along this journey of life.

To my grandparents for all the wisdom you've shared with me to help me learn, grow and change into who I am today.

To all the everyday heroes out there. May you save the world in a small way every single day.

HALLOWEEN 2024

ASPEN

"Bye Mom and Dad. I hope you have fun on your cruise," I said.

"Love you, Aspen. Have fun trick-or-treating," Mom said, pulling me in for a hug.

"Love you too," I said into her shoulder.

"Bye. Have a great couple weeks while we're gone and take good care of Pluto," Dad said.

"Will do. Love you, Dad," I said, as I pulled him in close for a hug.

I watched their car pull out of the driveway, and then they were off.

There's a chill in the air as the gentle breeze rustles the autumn leaves beneath my feet. Spooky music is playing down the street, and I can't help but smile as goosebumps trickle down my spine. The street is full of commotion as people walk from house to house. A slight hint of campfire smoke wafts in the breeze as golden hour approaches. I wander up my street and take a left at the corner.

I smiled and waved at my neighbors, the Martins, who were sitting on their front porch.

"I like your decorations," I said.

"Thank you, Aspen,"

"How have you been, Mrs. Martin?" I asked.

"Oh, please dearie, it's Mary to you. I've been good. I'm so excited for the Halloween festivities tonight. How about you?"

"Me too. I absolutely adore Halloween,"

"It's the best holiday of all time," Mrs. Martin said.

"Indeed. You have a good day now," I said, waving.

"Thank you. You too," Mrs. Martin said, waving back as I continued my way down the street.

I smile as I look around at the beautiful decorations and enjoy the lively hustle and bustle of people around me prepping for Halloween night. I shivered as a cold breeze blew my hair around my face and looked forward to the night.

One house has skeleton arms and legs in our yard. Another house has a whole skeleton dressed like a pirate sitting on the front porch. The older man who sits next to his pirate skeleton friend handing out candy is dressed like the skeleton's twin. Large groups of kids gather around him as he hands out the best candy on the street in addition to his wife's famous caramel apples which usually go fast.

Knock. Knock. Knock.

The brown front door opens, and I grin when I see his costume. He's wearing a skeleton shirt, black pants, and a skeleton mask. His blonde hair has been slicked back, and his brown eyes meet mine as he takes his skeleton mask off.

"Hi. I could smell the campfire all the way down the street," I said smiling.

Something seemed different with William than usual. I couldn't put my finger on what it was.

"I'm glad. It's nice and toasty," William says, walking towards the basement door, with me following close behind.

"After you," he said, opening the door.

"Thanks!" I said, as I ran down the basement stairs and out the patio door to his backyard.

"This looks like it came out of a movie, William! It's so spooky!" I said, as I looked around.

"Thanks. My mom was going for something like *Hocus Pocus* or *Halloweentown*,"

"Where did she get her ideas from?" I asked.

"Pinterest."

"That makes sense," I said, walking towards the garden.

Lights are strung up the trellis that leads into his mom's garden. Little lanterns are stuck into the ground to light the path that leads through the garden. Stepping stones are placed on the path. Peas and cabbage are growing to my right. To my left, violets, pansies and chrysanthemums are blooming. Scattered all around the yard are jack-o-lanterns, gravestones, and remnants of a skeleton here and there.

"Your mom did a great job on the decorating," I said, as William and I head over to the campfire area.

"You should tell her," he said, smiling.

"I will. Where are your parents by the way?" I ask.

"They're inside eating dinner. David had an evening swim meet today. They'll be out soon. Then, I told Fernando that we'd go trick or treating with him,"

"I'm glad. I can't have Halloween without trick or treating,"

"Same here. How have you been?" William asks, raising an eyebrow.

"Good, and busy with homework. I am looking forward to November,"

"Me too. I didn't think that senior year would be so intense," The door to the deck opens and William's mom calls, "Hi Aspen!"

"Hi," I responded.

"I made some pumpkin bread today. Do you want some?" William's mom asks from the top of the deck stairs.

"Yes, please. I love your baked goods. They always taste *sooooo* good."

"Thanks hon. I'll be back out in a minute,"

"How has AP Literature been going?" William asks.

"It's fine, I guess," I said, shrugging, "My favorite book so far has to be *The Grapes of Wrath.*"

"That's my favorite so far too. I like the imagery and the book." The door opens again, and William's mom followed by Fernando walk down the deck stairs. He pushes up his face with his pointer finger as he approaches

William and me.

"Hi Aspen!" Fernando says, "I'm so glad you're here,"

"I'm happy to see you. I heard we're going to go trick-or-treating soon,"

"Yes. I love candy!" He said, smiling from ear to ear.

"Same here, dude!" I say smiling while we do our secret handshake. We high five up high, down low, then in the middle then wiggle our fingers after the high five in the middle.

Fernando laughs.

"Here's your pumpkin bread," William's mom says, kindly.

"Thanks!"

"What time do you all plan to be done trick-or-treating?" William's mom asks as a strong gust of wind plays with the flames of the fire. I shivered and lingering tension hung in the air around us.

"Ten?" William asks.

I nod.

"Sounds great. I brought a bag out for each of you to put candy in. Have fun!" She said, waving.

Another strong gust of wind blows the brightly colored leaves around us. William's mom heads inside and I look up at the slightly cloudy sky and fog nearby, though we weren't near any water. *I hope the clouds go away soon.*

I sniffed the air and made a face.

"Do you smell that?" I asked.

"Yes," William said, while Fernando nodded.

"What is it?"

"I think someone burned something or has rotten eggs in their pantry," I said.

The air randomly went cold, then went back to being warm again. *Weird.*

William, Fernando, and I headed towards the gate which separates the yard from the street. We headed towards the house with the pirates first. By now, it's entirely dark except for the streetlights that have started flickering every time the wind picks up. Chills run down my spine as another gust of wind whips my ponytail this way and that.

"Are you all sure that the weather looks okay for tonight?" I asked.

"Yes," William and Fernando said in unison, yet their faces told a whole different story. I saw the worry lines etched in between their eyebrows and the slight worry in their eyes.

"Guys, look," I said, pointing to something that looked like a white sheet floating in the sky above us.

"That's only our imagination, right?" Fernando asked, slightly frightened.

"Pinch me," William said as Fernando pinched him.

"Ow."

"We're not dreaming then," I said.

"This is so creepy," Wiliam said, shivering.

"It wouldn't be Halloween without the spookiness," I said, winking.

The town is nicely decorated with jack-o-lanterns on every doorstep lit with candles inside. The full moon illuminates the cobblestone streets, brick houses, and historic plaques on the houses. Some houses were engraved years when they were first built, adding to the old charm of the town.

Each old house has a flowerbed nearby, adorned with beautiful blooming flowers. Some houses have a bird bath in their front yard, while others have windchimes that play a song every time the chilly evening wind blows.

We stroll down street after street chatting while we trick-or-treat. The moon shifts ever so slightly in the sky as we continue to walk down street after street. Trick or treating was a blur of many people opening their door to welcome using and handing us candy then we would continue on our merry way. Other houses had a dog that jumped at the window and barked loudly whenever we walked by. Some houses had creepy vampires that would jump out at us as we walked up the stairs to the front door. We chat for hours and before long, our feet begin to ache from all the walking and our costumes begin to feel itchy as they rub against our skin. By about ten, we were all tired and started to head home.

"Let me find a data connection," William said.

"Data connection lost," Siri said as the air around us went cold, then became humid.

William let out a heavy sigh and stomped in frustration. He angrily tapped the screen, trying to adjust his settings to get a data signal.

"Shoot," William said.

"Look at the streetlights," I said, worry lines etched between my eyebrows. All the streetlights up and down the street were as dark as the sky except for one that seemed to flicker.

"Doesn't it feel like someone's watching us?" I asked, chills running up my spine.

"Yes," William said, shivering, "Salem Massachusetts is giving me the creeps,"

"Same. I don't remember the last time I felt this creeped out," I said.

"Great, now we're really lost and there's no power and there might be someone watching us," Fernando said, panicked.

"It'll be okay," I said, attempting to calm Fernando down.

To our right was a mansion painted white with an iron fence built around the perimeter. To the right-hand side of the mansion was a garden. The sign in front of it read "Ropes Mansion," Of all the windows, the bottom right window was illuminated and the strange smell we smelled before came back for an instant, stronger this time, then it was gone.

"Look," I said pointing at the window, as this night began to feel more surreal to me than ever before.

"If the power's out in our neighborhood, how is that light on?" Fernando asked, running his fingers though his hair.

"What if it's haunted?"

"This place hasn't had inhabitants since 1907," I said, reading off the plaque on the gate.
"Wait. Stop talking. Listen," William said.

We all listened for a minute to piano music that played a lively tune somewhere nearby us.

"Where is that piano music coming from?" Fernando asked.

"Look," William said, pointing to the bottom right window of the Ropes Mansion.

Sure enough, there was a piano that played by itself. A select few keys were pressed down on either side of the piano, some notes high, and some lower. The music seemed to ring in the air around us, feeling foreboding as the song became faster and faster. It felt like there was some lingering message the song was trying to tell us. My heart raced as I tried to figure out the message behind the notes.

My palms were sweaty as I recognized the next tune: Braham's Lullaby. The irony of the song was that I was anything but sleepy right now, yet as the notes continued to play all the nostalgic memories of my childhood seemed to come back to me. I remembered reading books before bed, playing with my toys, and eating macaroni and cheese made by my mom after playing hide and seek. A younger version of myself ran around the house playing tag with my best friends while we all laughed and had a fun time. The stars would come out and we would lay on the grass staring up at them in awe and wondering about the beauty of the vast world above us. I felt connected to every single chord and note as the vibrations rang in the air and reverberated in my chest.

"Are you okay, Aspen?" Fernando asked, in a tiny, soft voice.

"Yes," I said, blinking as a tear rolled down my cheek, "Just lost in nostalgia,"

"Me too," William said, wiping his eyes as well.

When I looked over at him, I saw that he too looked solemn while listening to this lullaby.

After the end of the Lullaby, the piano playing abruptly stopped, and the window at the bottom right of the mansion shattered as a white bead of light came rushing out of it and disappeared into the air.

"Did you all see that?" William asked.

"Yes," William and Fernando said at the same time.

"Then, this mansion is probably haunted, which is why we need google maps to start working," William said, frustrated.

The wind picked up again and this time brought a downpour of rain with it.

"Oh great," William said, "Now I can barely see my phone,"

My palms started sweating as the light in the mansion began to move from the bottom right window towards the front door. From what I could see, there was a floating lit candlestick, which no one was holding.

"You guys, we really should get going," I said.

Not so fast, the breeze seemed to whisper within the rain. *Don't you want to stay?*

"Did you all hear that?" I asked.

"Yes."

We took off running wherever our legs would take us. Somewhere, anywhere away from this allegedly haunted mansion. Rain pelted us as we ran farther and farther. A flash of lightning illuminated the skies, and a boom of thunder rapidly followed.

"We need to get inside," Fernando said, "I don't care where."

"Gulu Gulu cafe is on the right. Let's go in there."

We ran up to the cute cafe as fast as we could.

"They're closed," William said, as he tugged on the door.

"It looks like everyone around here is closed," I said.

"Let's wait out the storm and power outage underneath this awning," Fernando suggested.

"Great idea."

All three of us, wet, scared teens sat down and waited as we caught our breath.

"I'm always going to remember this Halloween," I said, over the pouring rain.

"And not in a good way," Fernando said, running his fingers though his hair.

"Well, it depends on how you look at it. In some ways, to some people that are not the three of us, this could be a dream come true," William said.

"Yeah. It feels like we're inside of a Halloween movie," I said as thunder boomed.

"So right."

As we continued talking, the storm eventually cleared, and the rain lightened up. The streetlamps came back on, and we got a cell signal back on our phones. William had missed many worried texts from his mom, and I had missed many texts from my parents about where I was and why I wasn't home by curfew. At my house the curfew was midnight every night. My parents made sure I knew there would be big consequences if we failed to meet curfew expectations.

"We'd better get back home," William said, "Our parents are worried sick, lil bro,"

"I know. I've gotten the same messages you have. I wonder if they're still awake,"

"I'll follow you home," I said as a text came through from my mom. It read:

PLEASE STAY SAFE. I DON'T WANT YOU WALKING BACK HOME IN THIS WEATHER. THIS IS ONLY A SHORT BREAK IN THE STORM. WE HAVE ANOTHER ROUND COMING. STAY THE NIGHT AT WILLIAMS HOUSE AND YOU CAN WALK HOME IN THE MORNING. PLEASE TEXT ME WHEN YOU'RE ON YOUR WAY.

"My mom wants me to stay the night at your house. Is that okay?" I asked.

"Yeah," William said, "We'll find somewhere for you to sleep,"

"Thank you!" I exclaimed.

"Why does your mom want you to stay with us?" Fernando asked.

"The weather. It's a thirty-minute walk for me to get home and she'd prefer me to stick with you all and walk home in the morning," I said.

"Makes sense."

I heard a bell ringing in the distance and started counting. *One. Two. Three. Four. Five. Six. Seven. Eight. Nine.* Nine tolls of the bells.

"My goodness! How is it midnight already?" William said, hysterically.

He pulled out his phone to map us the rest of the way back to his house.

"It's a ten minute walk home. Let's get moving," William said.

"According to the radar, another wave of the storm is going to hit us in ten minutes. We'd better walk fast," I said.

In the sprinkling rain, we briskly walked down street after street, taking a few turns here and there until we walked by the Ropes Mansion which now had two windows lit up, possibly by candlelight. Then, at the end of another street sat William and Fernando's house, only a short walk away from the eerie Ropes Mansion.

"We're going in through the garage," William said as he punched in the code. We followed him like ducklings inside his house. His dog greeted us as we tiptoed into the kitchen. A light was on in the family room.

"Hello," a voice said from the family room.

Williams' face scrunched up in frustration. By just that action, he said, *I tried hard not to be caught and failed.*

"Hi mom," William said, soaked and dripping on the kitchen floor. We stood behind him like bodyguards, also dripping.

"I was worried sick. I'm so glad you're okay. What happened?" William's mom asked walking up to us, and taking William, then Fernando in her arms.

"Well……. we were out trick or treating when this storm hit and we had to find shelter somewhere. We found an awning to wait out the storm and before we knew it the clock struck midnight. And then we came straight home," William said.

"Yes, well let's get you all in some dry clothes then we'll talk more. Please dry up your puddle as well."

"Aspen, honey, would you like to stay the night? We have plenty of guest rooms,"

"Yes please," I said as I followed Fernando and William up the carpeted stairs.

After we were all changed into dry clothes, we gathered in the living room. William's mom made us brownies and lit a few candles for us in the living room. Thunder boomed once more.

"Come on over, enjoy your brownies and milk and then head to bed soon," William's mom, Mrs. Lowell commanded.

"Thank you!" I said, gratefully as I sat down on the couch in their living room next to a lavender vanilla scented candle.

"I'll be in my bedroom if you need me."

"Good night. Love you!" William and Fernando said.

As we sat in the living room on the couch and the storm continued outside, I could not help but think about how this was the spookiest Halloween I've ever had.

We gathered together on the couch and watched *Halloweentown*. As the movie played, I got lost in the scenes and the story line and my eyelids became heavy as I took small bites of brownie. I put my head on William's shoulder, and we relaxed into the serenity of watching a movie late at night. I struggled to not give into the sandman that beckoned me to come into dreamland. Fernando was already asleep about ten minutes into the movie, and I don't think I was long after him. CRASH! THUD! SCREAM!

I could practically hear William's rapid heartbeat as we both jumped at the jarring noises that seemed to echo throughout the house. Fernando jolted awake and I could see the terror in his eyes.

"Where did that come from?" Fernando asked.

"Upstairs, I think," William said, his face scrunched up in terror.

"MOM?" Fernando called up the stairs, running his fingers through his rumpled hair.

No answer other than another muffled scream.

"Grab a saucepan," William whispered to me.

"Where are they?"

"Under the sink, bottom left," William whispered.

Creek. Creak. Creak.

As we stepped on the floor, every footstep seemed to echo. *I hope there isn't an intruder in Fernando and William's house. What if there is, and they're just waiting for us to come upstairs to trap us in a room. What if....*

We tiptoed up the stairs, William going first, then me, then Fernando. Suspensefully slowly, we made it up the stairs and down the hallway. No noise was coming from William and Fernando's parents' bedroom. I thought I smelled smoke while we were walking up the stairs and when William kicked open the slightly cracked door to their parents' bedroom, my suspicions were confirmed. A fire had been started in the fireplace with five logs and beside the logs, a pink petticoat was lit on fire which caught the wood floor on fire. The smoke alarms started blaring. William's mom was gone. The window had been shattered as well as a glass candelabra with lit candles.

We all started coughing from the smoke and ran downstairs and out of the house.

Not so fast. A breeze seemed to whisper in my ear.

"What?" I asked.

"I didn't say anything," William said.

When I pulled on the front door, it didn't budge.

"Push," William commanded, and it opened.

"I'll call 911," I said.

William was so angry, terrified, and scared that he rapidly wiped tears from his cheeks.

Fernando gave a hug as his chest silently shook. Smoke billowed out the windows as rain continued to fall. Not as rapidly as before.

"Your call has been forwarded to voicemail. Please call back at a later time," *Beep.*

"They must not have power restored quite yet," I said, letting out a breathy sigh.

I held out my arms for William to cry into and he did. I held him until he took a solid deep breath and spoke without his voice shaking. It felt like an eternity until he felt well enough to make sense of his emotions. Fernando, watching his brother, also started crying silent tears.

"What are we going to do?" Fernando asked, his voice unsteady.

"I don't know yet. Come here. We'll be okay," I said, opening my arms for the boys to cry into.

"We'll figure something out, bro," William said.

"I can't believe this just happened," Fernando said.

"Me too."

"We lost our house and our mom on the same day. Why is the universe plotting against us?" Fernando said, shakily.

"Somedays, we are all thrown curveballs, yet it's how we react to the curveballs that matters," I said.

"That's wise. Thank you," William said.

"You're welcome. What do you need, right now?" I asked, pulling back to look at their

red, blotchy tearstained faces.

"I need time, and space," William said.

"Me too," Fernando whispered, trying to calm his breathing down.

"Okay. I guess we should wait until the streetlights come back on, then we can call the police to search for your mom," I said, "I'm always here if you need anything."

"Thank you," William said, for both of them and I could see the gratitude in their eyes.

"Look, the streetlights are on," Fernando whispered, shakily.

"You're right. I'll call again," I said.

When I called 911 again, they, sure enough, picked up and sent a firetruck our way. Their estimated time of arrival was around 1:45a.m. We wandered up to the end of the street, away from the smoke and waited for them to arrive. Just like that, we were soaked again. The thunder and lightning had passed, but the rain seemed content on continuing though the early morning hours.

"Where's your dad?" I asked.

"He's traveling for work. I should call him," William said.

I sat and listened to Williams call.

"Okay……. Yes……. Yes," William said, as he listened to his dad.

"Okay, so my dad is making a hotel reservation for us as we're still minors at the Salem Inn," William said, covering the speaker of his phone.

"Okay. Love you, bye," William said, before hanging up.

"We need to find our way to the Salem Inn. Our Dad is in California for work and told us he would call us back in the morning,"

"I'm so lucky he had his ringer on," William said, "I don't know what we would have done if he didn't pick up."

The fire trucks arrived and stopped where we were seated on the curb. William walked up to the firefighter who was driving the truck, asked him a few questions and came back.

"What a nice man," I said, smiling in the darkness of the cloudy, dreary, rainy night.

"Yes. I have his contact info, which I'll send to my dad in the morning."

"Let's go get some rest," William said, clicking the buttons to map us to Salem Inn.

As we followed William down the street, everything around us felt eerily quiet except for the rain pitter pattering on the sidewalks.

"I've heard some interesting stories about Salem Inn," Fernando said.

"What kind of stories?" I asked.

"Rumor has it that items disappear during the night in Room 17," Fernando said.

"Where have you heard these rumors?"

"School. Everyone talks about the Salem Inn and how it's haunted,"

"Interesting."

This walk felt *toooo* quiet. Around five minutes later when we arrived at Salem Inn, William opened the brown front door of the large red brick building to reveal a candlelit front room.

"Hello. Is anybody here?" Fernando asked.

A door creaked on its hinges.

"Anybody?" I asked.

Whoosh! An icy breeze blew through the front room. The wooden door behind the front desk opens and slams shut revealing an older man, with long white hair, a long white beard and a stocking cap.

"Hi. We wanted to check in for our stay," I said.

"Right this way," The man said grumpily.

He held a lantern in his right hand as he took a right from the front lobby and wandered down a hallway, took another right and ushered us into a room with the door propped open.

"W Seventeen," The old man read as he took note of where we would be for tonight in an old, tattered coffee-stained notebook.

"Breakfast is from 9am-11am in the lobby. Don't be late. Checkout is at 11:30 or earlier," he said.

"Thanks!" Fernando said.

Something about this man struck me as weird. I couldn't put my finger on what.

"Have a good night or shall I say have a spooky witching hour," The old man said with a cackle.

"Will do. Goodbye!" I said, slowly closing the door on the old man outside our room.

"I hope this room came with bathrobes," I muttered under my breath.

"Me too," William said.

"I'm so tired of being wet and cold," Fernando said.

Fernando was the first person in the shower. As soon as he was done, he collapsed onto a bed sprawled out diagonally and was immediately lost in dreamland. I went next in the shower, put my bathrobe on and climbed into bed. While William was in the shower, I lit a fire in the fireplace and hung up our soaked clothes to dry. I climbed into bed and left the bedside light on as I updated my mom in the form of a long text message about the events that occurred over the past few hours. I promised myself I would call to explain in the morning. William opened the door to the bathroom just as I finished typing my message and hit send. I was asleep within minutes.

Inside my parents' bedroom, a fire is lit in the fireplace crackling every few seconds, warming my hands, and toes. I walk downstairs to grab something to eat. My mom is upstairs getting ready for a ball she's going to soon. She's wearing a bright pink dress. I have an orange in my hand and my nimble fingers begin to peel the orange. I am sitting at the kitchen table enjoying the citrus scent of the orange as it's peeled when I hear a whisper within the air, "not so fast," Mom is screaming. Smoke is billowing down the stairs. Dad's heavy footsteps are running rapidly towards their bedroom. Dad had been outside doing work in the yard and was drenched in sweat. Mom's screams echo down the stairs as I run up them and see my mom, her bright pink petticoats on fire. She's screaming in pain. I want to run to her, pull her out of the fire and rescue her, but something is holding me back. Maybe not something but someone. "DAD! LET ME GO!" I say, tears blurring my vision.

Someone is nudging me.

"William. William. William. Wake up!" I said.

William wakes up panting and drenched in sweat.

"Are you okay?" Fernando asked.

"I will be," William said.

"You were screaming something about Dad and frantically rolling around in the bed," Fernando said.

"Just give me a minute," William said, taking shaky breaths, still panting.

I looked at my watch and it was 8am, so I padded my way to the window to open the curtain and let some daylight in. I sighed. This was going to be a long day. I felt our clothes which were dry by now. After we were all dressed and ready for breakfast, we took the long way around the Salem Inn to the lobby. The layout of the first level west wing was a square.

Step. Step. Creeeeaaakkk. Step Step. Creeeeaaakkkk. Meow! Meow!

"Did you hear that?" I asked.

"Yes. Sounds like a cat lives here. Great. Just another thing to creep us out!" Fernando said, crankily.

As we walked through the hallway I noticed the wall-mounted candelabras were lit and the carpeted hallway had red and green swirly patterns on it. The outside perimeter of the Inn had large windows, so daylight or moonlight could stream in. We found our way to the lobby to find the same older man who had checked us in standing behind the front desk.

I nodded at him as we walked towards the serving table. He nodded back, and checked new guests in. The table had an assortment of breads, eggs, waffles, pancakes, fruit, guacamole, arugula, and tomatoes. I filled my plate with pancakes, syrup and fruit, and saved a table for us.

When William and Fernando had made it through the breakfast line, they came over to the table with full plates. William had a stack of waffles, syrup, two hard boiled eggs, and a hash brown patty with ketchup. Fernando had a bagel with cream cheese, two hard boiled eggs, arugula, tomatoes, and fruit.

"If you can't tell, breakfast is my favorite meal of the day," Fernando said.

"Mine too," I said.

"So, we should discuss a few things about where we should go from here," William said, worry lines etched between his eyebrows.

"I'll call my dad later today hopefully before we check out from this hotel about the things regarding our family. Aspen, I'd like to know when you're planning on arriving home?"

"I don't know," I said, checking my phone for new messages from my mom. I didn't see any new messages from my mom; however, I did see a notification, and the reality crashed over me.

"Oh shoot!" I said, "My parents are on a cruise right now. I should be home right now watching our dog."

"In some ways that's a good thing though because you don't have people physically waiting at your house that you have to depend on," William said.

"Wait… so does that mean we can stay at your house until we find something to do about our house?" Fernando asked.

"I'll ask my mom," I said, pulling out my phone and typing a message.

HI MOM! I HOPE YOU HAVE A GREAT DAY ON THE WATER TODAY! HAS PLUTO BEEN FED? ALSO, WILLIAM AND FERNANDO'S HOUSE BURNT DOWN YESTERDAY AS A RESULT OF SEVERE WEATHER. CAN THEY STAY WITH ME AT OUR HOUSE FOR A FEW NIGHTS, PLEASE?

I was surprised when my mom responded almost instantly.

HI ASPEN! IT'S SO GREAT TO HEAR FROM YOU! HOPE YOU'RE DOING OKAY. PLUTO HAS BEEN FED. YES. OUR HOUSE IS THEIR HOUSE. PLEASE MAKE THEM FEEL AT HOME.

"You guys, guess what?" I said, smiling.

"What?" Fernando asked.

"You're staying with me at my house at least until your dad gets home from his business trip!"

"That sounds great!" William said.

"Let's go to your house after we're done with breakfast," Fernando suggested.

After breakfast was finished, and we had checked out with the same spooky older man as before, we ventured out into the streets of Salem, MA. I had the maps pulled up on my phone to my house. We had a forty-minute walk from the Salem Inn to my house.

I couldn't help but appreciate the beautiful architecture of the Salem streets we walked down. Every house was painted a different, bright color. Some were even made of red brick. They all had identical window flower beds with blooming flowers. The intricate designs of historical markers on houses made this experience more purposeful and meaningful to me because I walked on the very ground that the people who at some point lived in those houses had walked on. I felt as though I was encapsulated in history.

"I'll follow you," William said, "I'm going to call my dad on the way,"

"Sounds good," I said.

Fernando and I walked silently as William called his dad to inform him of the events of last night.

After about ten minutes, William hung up the phone with his dad.

"I think we have a plan. I need to make one more phone call," William said.

I listened in on his phone call as I walked.

"Okay. I'm sure you're *dying* to know what I was just asking my dad and the firefighter about," William said.

Fernando started laughing. I cracked a smile.

"So, our house unfortunately has no remaining items. The fire consumed everything, unfortunately and the cost to rebuild it is greater than the cost to buy it firsthand. That only makes me more grateful we have this friendship. I don't know what we would do without you Aspen. Thank you for your support," William said.

"You're welcome. Anytime," I said, smiling warmly.

"The fire fighter is starting a rescue mission to find mom," William said.

"That's great. But that doesn't mean we should stop looking for mom either," Fernando said, his face pale.

"Yes. We should check on Pluto first though," I said, "I hope he didn't cause any trouble while we were gone. Why don't you call the police on the way?"

"Great idea," Fernando said, "I'm dialing 911 now. I'll ask if they can start searching for our missing mother,"

"Good. I really miss her," William said, still distraught from the events that had happened on Halloween.

After Fernando got off the phone with the police, he said, "The police at the Salem station will start an outlook search mission for our mother. They need to see a profile picture and want to interview us on what happened on Halloween night at the station,"

"Let's print out some pictures at my house and head over there after lunch," I said.

"Sounds good."

WILLIAM
Police Interview

"Hi. Is there an Officer Martin here?"

"Yes, right this way. He's expecting a William—"

"That's me," I said.

"Then you must be Fernando," The front desk clerk said, "Pleased to meet you,"

He shook both of our hands and led us down a hallway. We entered a door on the right side of the hallway where an officer sat at his desk typing. He looked up as he heard us approaching.

"Good afternoon, Officer Martin. I have William and Fernando here to talk with you,"

"Excellent. Please pop a squat and we'll get started," Officer Martin said, as Fernando and I took a seat in front of his desk.

Mr. Martin pulled out a piece of paper and a pen to take notes about our conversation.

"First, I have to say, I'm so sorry for the drama that occurred. It must be a lot all at once for both of you. You're young too, which makes this harder.

My eyes were brimming with tears. The experience of losing the house made me angry, frustrated, and sad all over again. The empathy warmed my heart that had to be strong during the day for the people I needed to be there for. Yet, this empathy chiseled away at my heart, changing me for the better. It was as if my heart was frozen in time, only focusing on the good, and the empathy was like sunlight that melted the ice.

I looked at Fernando and saw that he didn't even try to stop the flood of tears that dripped down his cheek. I blinked and the tears began to fall down my cheeks too.

"Do you need some tissues?" Officer Martin asked.

We nodded.

After Fernando and I were done blowing our noses and wiping our eyes, Officer Martin said, "If you are both ready, I'd like to begin the interview,"

"We're ready," I said, looking bravely at Officer Martin.

"Can you please recount the events that happened on Halloween night?"

We told him the whole story, and by the end of our account, Officer Martin looked solemn.

"Wow," he said, blinking rapidly.

"That's quite the story. Do you have any people you suspect might have taken your mom away?"

"No one I can think of," I said.

"Me either. The only people I can think of who would want revenge would be the deceased," Fernando said.

"Interesting point there. Why do you think that?" Officer Martin said.

"I read lots of ghost stories," Fernando said, "I don't think many of them are real."

"I wouldn't be so sure. I've heard some pretty spooky stories of supernatural activity happening around here. It's probably just your imagination,"

"What stories have you heard?" I asked.

"Things like that are meant to be kept confidential."

"Understood."

"What do you think the person or thing that took your mom was after?" Officer Martin asked.

"Typically, in the ghost stories I like to read, ghosts usually have some sort of unfinished business they have to attend to," William said.

"Assuming this was a person, not a ghost, what do you think they wanted from your mom?" Officer Martin asked.

"I don't know," William said.

"They wanted something. I can tell you that. A house doesn't just burn down because of nothing. That leads me to another question. Why do you think whoever took your mom away took her through the window and burned her dress, and burned your house?"

"I really don't know. I hope it has nothing to do with a conflict our family has against other family members."

"If it did, do you know of someone it could have been?" Officer Martin asked.

"No, we don't know much about our deceased family members," Fernando said.

"I'll have a crew of police go to your house and look at the remains of the fire. I'll let you know if there are any clues discovered at the scene," Officer Martin said.

"Thank you. We appreciate it," I said, relieved that someone understood us.

"You're welcome. I want both of you to know that not all heroes wear capes. Both of you for your heroic actions today are a hero because it takes courage to do what you did just now,"

"Thank you," Fernando said, smiling.

"You're welcome," Officer Martin said, smiling sympathetically. As I drove home, I said, "I can't believe how kind, and supportive everyone has been about this situation."

"I agree. It feels so nice to be understood by these people. Officer Martin was especially apathetic," Fernando said.

"Yes. He makes me think of a rock, something stable, and strong in this tough time," I said.

"Great analogy."

"Hi. We're back," Fernando called as I followed behind him.

"Welcome," Aspen said, "How was the interview?"

"Great. Thanks for asking,"

"Oh. I see you all picked up Chipotle on the way back," Aspen said.

"Yes. We got a little hungry on the way back," I said.

"We'll eat this while we print some pictures of our mom for the search mission," Fernando said.

"Did you want some Chipotle, Aspen?" I asked.

"Yes please," Aspen said.

"We got you a bowl with two taco shells on the side," I said, handing her the bowl.

"I hope you like it."

"Thanks."

"We'd like to go shopping for some clothes after we're done eating. Is it okay if we take your parents car?" I asked.

"Yes, of course. I'll grab the keys for you when we're done," Aspen said.

"Thank you so much," I said.

"You're welcome," Aspen said, with a smile.

ASPEN

After everyone had finished eating, I grabbed the car keys for Fernando and William.

"Here you go," I said, dropping the keys into William's hand.

"Thank you," He said.

"Drive safe."

As soon as the car had disappeared from my sight, I headed upstairs to grab an old, dusty blank journal which had pages of parchment. I ran my fingers along the pages and started to hum quietly at first and then louder and louder. Then chant, until the pages of the book began to turn by themselves as if the air around me had fingers flipping one page after another. I watched in wonder and awe.

Piano music seemed to play in the background as a quill appeared in midair and started to write in sweeping strokes. My thoughts were crystal clear as they were written on the old notebook and dried.

Send to Sandy Sandwoman.

I pressed my palm into the cover of the notebook as if there was a button to send the message. I reopened the journal, and all the ink had disappeared from the pages. The journal was stowed once more in the one spot my parents never looked: underneath my bed. I opened my closet and parted my dresses, moving some to each side, revealing a hidden wooden door my parents had never seen, which had a lock on it. This wasn't just any lock, it was a heart shaped lock which needed a key to be opened. The keyhole was located at the very bottom point of the heart. The gold shined in the daylight.

The locked door in my closet was something my parents had never seen or heard of. It was the only special connection I had to *Sandy Sandwoman* over the course of time. I thought back and remembered the first time my grandmother had visited this house. She and I were playing dress up in my room on Halloween night. She wore a witch hat, and I wore a witch dress.   "Abra Cadabra," A younger version of myself said, waving a wand.

"Poof!" Grandma said, playing along.

"You know dearie, there's special magic hidden deep inside of you. If you believe in it, you can discover so many great things."

"How do I discover my magic?" I asked, awestruck.

"Just close your eyes and imagine you have magical powers."

I closed my eyes. I heard whispering from somewhere nearby.

"Open them," Grandma Sandy said, moving my dresses to the side, revealing the door to me for the very first time.

"Wow. It's like *The Lion, The Witch and the Wardrobe,*" I said, excitedly. I ran over to it and ran my fingers along the door, and down the heart shaped lock. I pulled on the lock, nothing happened.

"How do I unlock it, Grandma?" I asked.

"In time, you'll find the answer in your heart," she said.

Now, I searched for the answer lingering somewhere in my heart.

Keys. Where are my keys?

I headed downstairs and opened the junk drawer by the refrigerator. I found an assortment of birthday candles, stamps, return address labels, pebbles and more. No keys. I looked on the hooks in the coat closet and found nothing. I looked at the hooks by the front door. Nothing.

I need my key.

I texted William: I'M HEADING TO THE ANTIQUE STORE.

As I walked down the street to the antique store in the neighborhood. I passed by a witch tour shop, and I couldn't help but go inside. I loved the jack-o-lantern masks in the window and the pointy black witch hats in the display case.

I poked around in the shop with cookbooks, stickers, Salem and MA shirts. I could have spent hours in that very shop, reading every cookbook with recipes for steaming elixir, pumpkin muffins, and pumpkin crepes. I found the shelf sometime later with plastic cauldrons of all sizes and I knew I couldn't leave this store without buying one.

I bought a small black pointy witch hat, and two cauldrons: one medium for stews, and soups and one for my keys. I continued down the street picking a few wildflowers along the way to put in my hair and looked down at my watch. I couldn't believe the time I saw. It was five o'clock, which meant I needed to get home to feed Pluto and whip up some dinner.

The daisy wildflower bounced up and down where it was behind my ear as I skipped home humming every step of the way. I loved the slight chill in the breeze and bright yellow leaves scattered all over the sidewalk as I danced and skipped. By the time I was home and unlocked the door Fernando and William had already arrived and were putting their new clothes in the washer.

"I'm home," I called.

"Hi. Welcome home," Fernando said, "I thought you were going to the antique store,"

"I was until I wasn't. I needed new keys but then I just happened to turn a corner, and this wonderful witch tour shop was right there. I couldn't help myself," I said.

"I'd say you couldn't. That's an impressive haul there!" William said, coming
down the stairs.

"Where do you plan to keep your cauldrons?" Fernando asked.

"By the hearth," I said.

"I like your new hat," Fernando said, "Did you buy it at the witch store as well?"

"Yes. I love this new hat too. It fits, doesn't it?" I said.

"Yes."

As I cooked dinner, Fernando and William sat in the living room playing checkers with the Freeform channel on in the background. I started cooking by warming broth up on the stove and gradually adding more food to the veggie broth. Orzo rice was added first, which quickly soaked up all the liquid and flavor, then canned diced tomatoes, then melted parmesan cheese, then frozen peas, and frozen corn. This was my favorite type of soup to make. I usually referred to it as a cheesy orzo date night stew. I added some spices, warmed a baguette in the oven and called the boys over to eat our steaming hot stew.

We said grace before starting to eat. I watched the steam rise from the stew as the heat warmed my fingertips and caused them to grow damp for just an instant. Then I wrapped my fingers around the soup bowl as if it was a mug. I felt instantly warm inside. I took off my hat and hung it on the chair while I ate.

"This is good," Fernando said.

"I'm glad you like it," I said.

"It's one of my favorites. I also made the sourdough baguette before the Halloween drama," I said, "I hope it's flavorful."

"It most certainly is. Did you add rosemary?" William asked.

"Yes, a touch of rosemary and salt."

"I like the twist on the classic sourdough recipe you pull off so well," Fernando said.

•

After we had all finished eating, and the dishes were stacked in the sink, I took William and Fernando upstairs to show them where they'd be staying for tonight.

"This is your room," I said, opening the door to the room which was painted blue on all four walls. It had no windows as it was on the back of the house which backed up to the forest. The queen-sized bed had a fluffy blue comforter on it and the pillowcases were white, soft and plush.

"I'll grab you some towels," I said, "Let me know if there's anything else I can do to make your stay more enjoyable."

"Thank you, Aspen," William said, belly flopping onto the fluffy, cloudlike mattress.

"You're welcome. Just one thing to ask of you both,"

"Okay."

"Never look in the closet. It's off limits," I said, wagging my finger in a no-no gesture.

"Why?" William asked, eyebrow raised.

"This is no time to ask questions," I said, "You both are surely very tired and need some sleep."

"Very right," Fernando said, yawning.

I exited the room and left the door cracked.

I went downstairs and started digging through drawers again in hopes of finding the key. I started by the refrigerator and dug through stamps, candles, random scraps of paper, paper clips, and so much more. I came up empty. *Okay. I guess I'll try another drawer.* The next drawer to the right was the silverware drawer. I pulled this drawer out and looked under all the silverware, digging through every utensil until I came up empty once again. *It never takes me this long to find my keys.*

I started digging through a third drawer, a fourth drawer and a fifth drawer until I started dumping everything out on the kitchen floor, digging through everything. No key. My heart raced as I entertained a scenario in my mind. *What if there was no key? What if this was all a trick? No. That can't be the case. Surely there had to be a key, right?*

I poured out three more drawers, dug through the contents, let out a frustrated sigh and sat down on the cluttered kitchen floor. I didn't care about the mess around me. *Sandy, please help me find this key. I'm desperate.*

After what seemed like hours of searching on a tired body, I headed upstairs to find the parchment paper book open on my bed, glowing green, then red, then blue, then a blinding bright yellow until it closed, and darkness was the only thing left behind.

And only one word rested on my lips, "Sandy,"

Tap. Tap. Tap.

I recognized the rhythm of the taps immediately. I opened my window, looked to the moon, and tapped the exact same rhythm back until a bottle appeared on the windowsill. It was filled with a sparkly powder of sorts. The label read: *Stardust. Use sparingly. Dreams occur within a minute of use.*

I sighed and whispered, "Thank you Sandy" into the chilly night air.

•

Footsteps were heard somewhere close by as the floor creaked with every step making the house feel ancient with every creak. Someone was walking down the stairs. I rushed down the stairs behind them. I immediately recognized the beachy blonde hair as Williams.

"William. William," I said, tapping him on the shoulder. He was one step below the stairs I was on.

"What?" he asked, agitated.

"Where are you going?" I asked, curious.

"To the kitchen. Can't sleep," he said.

"Why don't I make you a warm beverage and bring it up to you?" I said.

"Why can't I just do it myself?" He asked, slowly growing more frustrated

"Because I want to do something nice for you," I said.

"Okay. Go ahead. I'll be in my room reading."

Silence.

"Aspen?"

"Yes."

"What was all the banging and crashes I heard earlier?"

"No need to worry about that. Everything's fine," I said, dancing around the truth.

"No - really what were you doing?"

"I think you need a nice long rest, and we can discuss this in the morning. Your warm beverage will be delivered shortly. Off you go, up to your room," I said.

Stardust Sleepy Elixir

Ingredients:
Raw cherry juice (8 ounces)
Honey (1 tablespoon)
One pinch stardust
Chamomile tea (8 ounces)

Warm all ingredients except the stardust in a small pot on the stove allowing tea to steep for 4 minutes. Add stardust at the end to brighten the color of the beverage and induce slumber.

Warning: Any time an ingredient in this beverage is used too much or too often, there could be side effects. Be careful when and how you use this beverage.

I carried the beverage upstairs to William and handed it to him.

"Here you go."

"Thank you!"

"You may want to climb into bed with that beverage. I've heard it induces slumber quickly because it has tart cherry juice," I said.

"I've heard about the health benefits of tart cherry juice and never tried it before,"

"Try it," I encouraged.

William took a sip.

"It's good. Sort of tangy, yet sweet at the same time."

"I thought you'd like it."

"I do, very much. Can I have another one of these tomorrow night?"

"Yes," I said, secretly elated he liked it.

"I'm going to head to bed," William said, yawning.

"Great idea."

I heard William snoring loudly within minutes and headed downstairs to dig through everything on the floor to find keys. I had no luck whatsoever. So, I opened the door and headed outside into the chilly, crisp night air on a mad search for keys.

WILLIAM

Dream: Morning

I'm walking down a dark, streetlight lit street towards a white mansion on a rainy evening. Every cold raindrop makes me shiver. The rain is consistent, yet a calming noise until I hear a rustle from the trees - A crow. This crow swoops around me and grabs a stick from nearby, lays it on the ground and begins to spell out something on the ground. He spells out: A – N – G – U – S.

"Hi there," I mouth.

No sound comes out though.

Crows fly above me. They're trying to say something to each other, yet I can't pick up what it is until I see one particular crow which I recognize. It's as if something clicks when I see this crow and their song is loud and clear. Their message has dawned on me as they stare at me with big, black beady eyes. *Trust the universe. It will guide you to where you need to be. Right here, right now.*

I continue walking. My boots feel heavy as water begins to pool inside. I arrive at the white mansion at the end of the street, soaking wet, dripping. I knock three times. The extremely white, almost ghostly looking butler opens the door and welcomes me inside. Only one window is lit in this mansion: the upper right. I pour the water out of my boots on the porch before walking inside, leaving a puddle beneath me. I have goosebumps all the way up my arms and legs. Prickles crawl up my back as I stand in the entryway.

"I'll grab you a towel sir," The butler seems to mouth at me.

For what seems like hours, the mansion is freezing cold and I'm shivering until the butler returns with a towel and a robe for me to put on after drying off.

"Fire," He mouths to me, and disappears down the hallway.

I follow him down the dimly lit hallway. He seems to be floating, not walking down the hall, up the stairs, and into the lit room.

"Fire," He mouths again, almost urging me to get closer to it. Chills prickle down my spine.

"Not so fast," He mouths as I take a step forward. He snaps his white transparent fingers, and a face appears in the fire. He disappears.

First, I hear agonized screaming from this face. Then, I look closer and see who the screaming face in the fire is: my mom.

"Mom," I try to say. No sound comes out.

Her lips say something. I can't read it.

"What?" I mouth back to her.

She mouths what she's trying to say again and again until I pick up on what she's mouthing.

I'm still here. Alive.

I wake up, my heart racing, a bead of sweat on my forehead slowly rolling down my face.

Why can't I ever sleep?

Fernando, next to me, seemed to be sleeping peacefully and I wished I could sleep like he could. *Why do I keep having these dreams? They never stop.*

Inhale. Exhale. It's okay. You can find sleep and calm here, right now.

After deeply breathing for a little bit, I found my way back asleep until morning.

Fernando poked me and I opened my eyes slightly.

"Do I have to wake up?" I asked.

"Yes. You do. You have to come see this!" Fernando said.

I crawled out of bed and Fernando, and I walked down the creaky stairs to the kitchen, which was a disaster.

"What was Aspen doing so late at night and why did she leave such a huge mess?" I wondered aloud.

"I don't know. I hate messes," Fernando said.

"She's gone crazy looking for something," I said.

"I wish we knew what she was looking for," Fernando said.

"Where is she by the way?"

"I don't know, but she left a note and a berry tart for us."

"Let me read it."

Crust Me Tart

Ingredients:
For the crust
1 1/2 cup (200g) all-purpose flour
1/2 cup (50g) powdered sugar
1/8 teaspoon kosher salt
1/2 cup plus 2 tablespoons (10 tablespoons or 140g)
unsalted butter, very cold, cut into 1/2-inch cubes
1 egg, lightly beaten
1/4 teaspoon vanilla extract

For the filling
1 cup (8 ounces) mascarpone cheese, room temperature
1/4 cup (60ml) cold heavy cream
1/3 cup (43g) powdered sugar
1 teaspoon orange or lemon zest
1/2 teaspoon vanilla extract
3 ounces (85g) raspberries
8 ounces (225g) blueberries
8 ounces (225g) strawberries, stems removed and halved
or quartered
4 tablespoons (60ml) apricot jelly or orange marmalade
2 tablespoons water
1 teaspoon red wine vinegar or lemon juice

1) Make the tart dough:

In a food processor, add the flour, powdered sugar, and salt. Pulse a couple times to combine.

Add the cubed cold butter and pulse several more times until the largest piece of butter is the size of a pea.

Add the egg and vanilla extract. Pulse a few more times until the dough begins to form clumps and pull away from the side of the food processor.

2) Press the dough into the tart pan and freeze:

Lightly grease the inside of a tart pan (with removable bottom) with butter.

Dump the clumpy dough into the tart pan and spread out evenly with your fingers along the bottom and up the sides of the tart shell. You don't have to press too hard; if the dough is still a little crumbly, that's good.

To make the top even you can press the dough up a little higher than the tart pan edge and use a rolling pin over the top to even the edges.

Put the tart pan in the freezer for 1 hour.

3) Preheat the oven to 375°F.

Place the oven rack in the middle of the oven.

4) Pre-bake the crust:

Line the frozen tart crust with aluminum foil, with enough extra foil off two sides to use for lifting.

Fill with pie weights—dry beans or ceramic or stainless pie weights. Place a shallow baking pan on the bottom rung of the oven to catch drippings. Put the tart pan in the oven on the middle rack. Bake for 20 minutes. Remove from oven and remove the pie weights. (I lift the hot beans out by holding on to the aluminum foil and place the foil and beans into a large bowl to cool before storing.)

Poke the bottom of the crust with the tines of a fork. Return the tart pan to the oven for 10 to 15 more minutes. Bake until golden brown. Remove from oven and let cool completely.

5) Mix the filling ingredients, then spread into tart crust:

Using an electric mixer, beat together the mascarpone, cream, powdered sugar, orange zest, and vanilla extract on high speed until stiff peaks form, about 40 seconds to a minute.

Scoop the mixture into the tart crust and spread it so that it is level.

6) Arrange the berries on top, brush with jelly mixture:

Arrange the berries on top of the mascarpone mixture in the tart crust.

Combine the jelly or marmalade, water, and vinegar or juice into a small saucepan and heat on medium heat until bubbly and the jelly has dissolved as well as it can.

Using a pastry brush, brush the jelly mixture over the berries for a glossy sheen.

Remove the rim of the tart pan before serving. (You may need to use a knife to gently separate the edges of the tart from the pan.)

Store covered in the refrigerator for 1 to 2 days. To make

ahead, make the crust and filling and store covered in the refrigerator for 1 to 2 days. Add the fruit and glaze the day of serving.

Dear Fernando and William,

I have left this morning to run a few errands and pick up a few essentials. Should be back by dinnertime tonight. I hope you enjoy the homemade freshly made berry tart I made early this morning.

Your friend,
Aspen

"The tart is good, yet bittersweet," Fernando said, putting his fork down on his plate.

"You're right," I said, trying a bite.

"I can't believe she didn't make any comment about the mess in the kitchen in her note," Fernando said.

"Maybe she intends on cleaning it up later?" I said, hopeful.

"Yes. That would be fantastic," Fernando said.

"How would you like to spend our day?" I asked.

"We should eat some lunch and continue to search for our mom,"

"Yes. Good idea."

Knock. Knock. Knock.

"I don't know who's at our door, and who comes this early to drop off packages or mail?"

"Crazy people."

Knock. Knock.

"Coming."

I opened the door and recognized the man standing on the front porch immediately.

"You're from the Salem Inn, right?" I asked.

"Yes. You have not paid for your night at the Salem Inn. Here's an invoice that needs to be paid within the next 24 hours," he said.

"I swear the firefighter paid this for us. How did you find us?" I asked.

"I have my ways," he said.

I nodded.

"If you don't pay this bill in the next 24 hours, there will be consequences," He said, pointing a finger at the bill I held in my now sweaty hands.

"Okay," I heard my voice say and closed the door.

"I had a feeling something like this would happen," I said, pushing my back to the door.

"That firefighter was not trustworthy," Fernando said.

"Let's call Dad to see what next steps we should take,"

I pressed the call button for my dad's number. We listened to it ring for a few seconds, then hung up. Then, I tried again. And again - and this time he finally picked up.

"Hi Dad," I said, trying to sound calm.

"Hi. What's up?"

"You know how the firefighter said he would pay for our night at the Salem Inn?"

"Yes."

"He never paid it."

"I'll have to handle it when I get home," Dad said.

"We don't have that kind of time. The manager just stopped by Aspen's house and said we needed to pay within the next 24 hours otherwise there would be consequences,"

"Okay. I'll book a flight home soon. I'm taking sick leave to do this, and I'll be home within the next eight hours hopefully," Dad said, "Wait……. Are you staying with Aspen?"

"Yes. It's a long story. I'll tell you when you get home……… or I guess to Aspen's home,"

"Good idea. We need to search for Mom too. I'm worried about her," I said.

"Yes. Please ask Aspen if I can stay at her house when I get back."

"I will."

"I need to go talk to my boss about this. I'll talk to you later," Dad said.

"Thank you for coming home early. We appreciate it," I said.

"You're welcome. Bye. Love you."

"Love you too."

"I suppose, we'd better talk to Aspen about the mess in the kitchen when she gets home."

"And I think I hear her walking into the garage right now."

ASPEN

Twenty Hours Before

After William went to bed, I headed out into the crisp evening air wea
ring my favorite purple cloak, and my newest pointy hat. I wandered down a trail that would lead me to where I needed to go.

This trail wasn't just any trail though. It only appeared to the people who were worthy of discovering it. Only the universe knows a person is ready to discover this beautiful magical trail. When their heart and soul are ready, the path will be opened to them in a matter of time. Along the trail are moonlight berry bushes, night blooming fennel, blue moon basil, blood moon basil, night blooming nuts and so much more. These were the spices I grew up on that were almost like healing medicine for the soul. I inhaled and exhaled, and all the memories seemed to float in thin air within the darkness that surrounded me. I heard an owl in the distance start to hoot and it almost seemed to echo throughout the woods.

The sound sent welcome goosebumps down my spine. These weren't goosebumps of fear, rather goosebumps of pleasure almost like a sigh when everything seems to be right with the world. As I walked along this path further and further, I began to notice signs that indicated I was getting closer. The bumpy tree roots on the right side of the path. The blue post with a white sign hung on it. The constant, consistent switchbacks along this trail. I remembered the feeling of walking this many times as a kid, loving the joy that seemed to have me overflowing with happiness, imagining the face that would meet me at the end of the hike. I remembered the satisfaction of arriving, the brown door opening and inhaling the pine tree scent of the cottage lost in the woods at the tippy top of the hill.

I remembered playing with my older sister whom I missed dearly because she was away at college. We would play twenty questions many times as we wandered up switchback upon switchback, counting down the turns until we arrived, slightly sweaty, yet overjoyed because of the person we'd be seeing. The ghosts of memories lingered over me as I recognized everything that felt familiar in that moment. I heard the faint laugh of my older sister as she laughed at a joke I had made, and the smile in her voice that seemed to brighten me up as well.

I shook my head as if shaking the memory away and clearing my head in order to focus on what had to be done. I had to stay present and anchored to putting one step in front of the other, closer and closer to this house that seemed to be calling my name, from deep within me. *Aspen. Aspen. Aspen.* The breeze within the trees whispered to me, drawing me closer.

The blue house at the end of the trail was lit up with decorative white lights and had daffodils and daisies which I could only faintly see in the darkness. The house came into focus the closer I got to it. I lifted the brass door knocker of a woman in a nightcap, with a slight wart on the bottom right of her chin, eyes gently closed, ring hung in between her teeth. I let it fall back against the door exactly three times, then stepped back.

The half awake older lady opened the door and said, "Aspen?"

I held my breath and said, "Hi Grandma."

"Come on in," She said, "I've been watching over you in my crystal ball and I could sense you were coming. I'm so glad you're here! I have tea brewing for our time together. What brings you here at this time of night?"

"I need a story. I can't sleep and I need something soothing to imagine. I need a good dream."

"Before I tell you a story, why don't you tell me what's been going on? It's been a while since you've been here and you know I love to hear about everything."

As I tell her about all the Halloween drama with William and Fernando, she listens and stirs the soothing bedtime elixir round and round in the pot on the hot stove. Her stove top is black with dials on the side. She opens a wood finished cabinet to get out a white mug. The walls in her kitchen are a soothing shade of blue that makes me think of the ocean. As I talk, I watch her open a different cabinet. This second cabinet has a label written in black ink on a piece of parchment paper. It reads, "Stardust," Inside the cabinet are spice jars with powders of all different colors, textures, and appearances.

I pause in my storytelling when I realize I have told all there is to tell of my story. I only wished I had solutions to the problems.

"Grandma," I said.

"Yes, dear."

"What would you do if you were in my shoes?"

"Well……. Darling, that's hard to say. I think that as much as being independent is good for you youngins, you need an adult there to help you in times like these. You'll find wisdom that runs deep when you find and ask for help."

"Well said. I needed to hear that. Thank you for your wisdom, Grandma," I said, falling into a hug where I feel sheltered, safe and comfortable.

"You're welcome, Aspen, anytime. I love you."

We hugged and swayed back and forth for a little while until the timer started beeping, indicating my tea was done.

"I love you too," I said.

A calming silence rested over us as Grandma poured the dark red warm bedtime elixir into the white mug.

"Grandma," I said, once again as another question popped into my head.

"Yes, sweetie."

"What are all those Stardust's used for? I've only used one on William. I have yet to use all of them."

She opened the cabinet once again and read all her labels.

"That's your story for tonight. Let me go grab a few things to move this tradition forward,"

As my grandma wandered upstairs to find what she needed to help tell the story, I wandered into the family rooms, and the memory wave that crashed through my brain was so intense with emotion and shocked awe I stood there for a second letting the memories come to life.

A blonde-haired boy playing with Thomas the train on the floor. An older girl with black hair like mine, a slightly crooked nose, and glasses sitting next to him building more tracks. A blonde girl almost the same age as the blonde-haired boy rocking a little baby doll back and forth in her arms. A brown skinned boy with brown eyes folding a cardboard box and taping it to turn it into a starship. Little child voices, and minds eagerly imagining everything as they played in their own beautiful world, no worries about the real world. The only thing that mattered to them in that moment was to just be. Whether that meant being present while playing with their toys or with each other, all they needed to do was be themselves without thinking about what one another thought.

"Are you okay, dear?" Grandma asked behind me, causing me to jump.

"Yes," I peeped out, face solemn.

I blinked, as a tear dripped down my face.

"Really, what's the matter, dear?" Grandma asked, her face empathetic.

"The memories that surround this house. I can never go anywhere in this house without the memories following me around. I miss those times."

I blinked again, letting the big drops of salty water fall and drip.

"Come here," Grandma said, opening her arms for a hug. I fell right into it and focused on calming myself down. *Inhale. Exhale. Inhale. Exhale. You're okay.*

"Time for your story," Grandma said, leading me over to a rocking chair, sitting down and patting her lap. A younger version of me crawls right into the rocking chair, her foot on the ground rocks us back and forth and my breath synchronizes with the soothing rhythm of the rocking. The steam from the mug of my bedtime tea swirls in the air and I take a sip before placing it back on the end table.

"Once upon a time……," Grandma begins, still rocking me back and forth. I become lost in the lulling sensation and begin to drift away into dreamland.

I'm walking down Essex Street towards Ropes Mansion. It's a cloudy overcast day. A woman walks toward me coming the opposite way. She's blurry at first as the cloudy mist hovers over her, but when she comes into focus, I see it is my grandma.

"Hi," I mouth.

"Hi," She mouths back.

The whole conversation we seem to be having seems to be on mute. She's silently trying to tell me something. She repeats this again and again. I try to pick up what she's trying to say until my tired brain is exhausted. My eyes drop down to a gold chain she wears around her neck. The necklace is tucked into her shirt. I step closer, and tenderly, gently pull the necklace out of its hiding spot.

At the end of the chain is a golden key with the words inscribed on the handle: Trust your intuition. My grandma mouths her sentence another time, and this time I pick up what she's been trying to say this whole time. "The answer is in your heart. Believe in yourself,"

She takes her key back from my fingertips and hides it under her shirt and vanishes into thin air like a cloud evaporated by a ray of sunlight.

"No grandma, I need that key," I said, but there is no one around on this gloomy day to hear me.

I continued walking further and further down the street to Ropes Mansion. I trail my fingertips up the railing as I walk up the staircase to the door and knock three times. No answer. I try to turn the knob. Locked.

A chilly breeze rushes over me. "Not so fast. In time," Is the whisper I hear in the air. The chill vanishes as well as the mansion.

I woke up in my guest room at my grandmother's house. At some point I must have been carried up the stairs up to my room. I look at my alarm clock to see that it's nearly seven o'clock. A drop of sweat drips down my arm when flashes of my dream come back to me. *It's just a dream. It's just a dream. You're okay.*

Grandma is waiting at the bottom of the stairs for me.

"Hi Sleeping Beauty. Here's a basket of fresh berries for you to take home."

"Thank you, Grandma!" I said, warmed by her kindness.

"You're welcome. Just one more hug before you go," she said.

When I wrapped my arms around her, I thought for an instant I felt that golden chain I saw in my dream. I closed my eyes and pictured it perfectly, opened my eyes once again and there it was around her neck, tucked into her shirt. This was a detail I'd never noticed before. I'd always been too busy playing with my toys and having tons of fun. Now, I noticed the necklace which made me wonder: Was my dream really a dream?

ASPEN'S POV

Present day

"Hi! I'm home," I said.

"Aspen, thank goodness you're home," Fernando said.

"We have a bit of a situation," William said, entering the entry room behind him. He looked extremely tired, as if he hadn't slept in days. He had bags under his eyes, and a mug of coffee in his hand.

"Are you doing okay, William?" I asked, my eyebrows knitting together.

"Yes, just tired."

"Our Dad is tired of having to deal with all this drama long distance, so he's coming home by the end of the day today," Fernando said.

"Home as in where?" I asked.

"I don't know. I think he's going to stay at your house if you're okay with it for the first night and then, I don't know what we're doing," William said.

"We need you to take care of the tornado in the kitchen," Fernando said.

"Will do. First, I need to show you something in your room," I said.

"Ummm………. That's another thing," Fernando said, "We might have already opened the closet."

"What!?" I asked, my voice growing louder, "You were never

supposed to open the closet in the first place."

"We were so curious to know what was inside, and you weren't here to tell us no, so we opened it and found something," Fernando said.

"Show me," I said. A faint ticking slowly became louder as we headed up the stairs. When we finally walked into Fernando and Williams' guest room, the closet doors were wide open, and the room was dark except for a single ray of sunlight coming in through a small window that was built into the far closet wall. The window was about a square foot large, the light from the window shone onto a tiny tree that was only a matter of inches large. It had a miniature treehouse built on one of the branches, and little lanterns all throughout the tree. My guess was that at night the lanterns lit up, powered by the moonlight. This tree was planted in a small field of grass, which sat on a small table with four legs. Next to the tree was a pocket watch with the same heart lock the door in the closet had. The pocket watch never seemed to want to stop ticking.

Tick, tick, tick, tick.

"The ticking sound was driving us crazy this morning, so we followed the sound, and it led us here," William explained.

"I see. I recognize the lock. I have the same one," I said.

I walked toward my room with William and Fernando at my heels.

"Why do you think we have the same lock?" Fernando asked. William yawned.

"I don't know. What I do know is that your dad may be mad if the house is a disaster when he gets home. Do you mind helping me clean up?" I asked.

"Not at all," Fernando said.

William yawned again.

"I'm happy to help," William said, sleepily.

"Really, are you doing, okay?" I asked William.

"Yes. I haven't been sleeping well. Bad dreams."

We headed down to the kitchen together and I sighed when I saw the mess I'd made looking for keys.

"Do you see why I dug through all the junk drawers now?" I said.

"Yes. You needed to find the keys," Fernando said.

"I wanted to find them and was extremely unsuccessful. Let's put all this away in any open drawer and then we can look for keys," I said.

As we shoved all the miscellaneous things floating around on the floor and the counters into drawers, William sat and watched.

"When are we going to search for our mom?" he asked, arms crossed, tapping his foot on the ground.

"When your dad gets here?" I suggested.

"Okay. I'm just worried about her because she's out there somewhere. I have no clue where and I miss her. I want her to be back with us, so we can be together," he said, his voice cracking with emotion.

"I feel the same way, bro," Fernando said.

"I have a sneaking suspicion your dad is going to be here earlier rather than later. We might want to relock the closets, so your dad has nothing to be suspicious of. Let's try a different key on your pocket watch tonight after sunset."

We headed back upstairs to find the pocket watch right where we had left it. Now, it had a small message inscribed on the back written in tight, neat cursive. It read, *"Thyme to think about time."*

"Look at this message," I said.

"Thyme to think about time," William read, slightly squinting to read the small writing.

"I can't believe we missed this before," Fernando said.

"What do you think it means?" I asked, excitedly.

"What if we were to rewind time with this pocket watch to Halloween when mom was still here?" William said.

"Yes. Great idea. Then we could change what happened and make sure she doesn't go missing," Fernando said.

"But first, we need a key," I said, thinking.

"Meet me at midnight on the front porch. We'll go key hunting and hopefully be able to unlock the pocket watch before sunrise," I said.

"Wait… what about the thyme," Fernando asked.

"Whoever wrote this wouldn't give us a clue like this without adequately thinking it through," William said.

"I know where we need to go, and exactly what we need. It's important we all meet at midnight to do this," I said.

"But first…" Fernando said.

The doorbell rang.

"Dad's here," William said

"I will lock up the closets and tidy up the bedrooms," I said.

"We'll keep him busy downstairs," Fernando said.

"Okay. I'll cook dinner when I'm done up here," I said.

I locked William and Fernando's closet, trying to grab the locket off the table to carry with me tonight, but this time when I tried to lift it, it wouldn't budge. *Oh great. Now we're going to have to wait for the sun to go down a second night to rewind time unless we're back before the sun comes back up.* I locked up the closet and made William and Fernando's bed. As I did so, I noticed the puddle of dampness on the sheets on Williams' side of the bed. *Maybe it's more than just not sleeping well.*

I headed across the hall to my bedroom, looked at my book, which was open on the bed. A message in the book awaited me. It read: *Stardust story requested. Come again.* I closed the book, and it glowed green, then yellow, then blue. I pressed my hand to the center as a fire stirred up in my insides, a fire of anxious energy that needed to be put into something. I pressed my hand into the center of the book. *I let go. I trust. The answer is inside.* The book seemed to vibrate underneath my hand for a second and then it stopped glowing. I reopened it and saw a new message. *Turn to page 232.*

"Aspen," William called up the stairs.

"Yes," I called down.

"I need to know what to make for dinner."

"Coming," I called.

I closed the book, hid it under my bed, closed and locked my closet and headed downstairs to greet William and Fernando's Dad. He seemed familiar somehow.

"Hi," I said, shaking his hand.

"Hi Aspen. Nice to see you again," he said.

Again? Where did I know him from?

"Nice to see you too," I said, smiling.

Mr. Lowell was a tall, broad-shouldered man with black rimmed glasses, blue eyes and black hair.

"We're happy you're home Dad," William said, giving his dad a hug.

"I'm happy to be home, even if I need to miss some meetings."

Fernando joined in on the hug as I started to boil water to make tortellini. I warmed some canned tomato sauce on the stove and added one can of diced tomatoes to make it juicer.

"So, tell me more about this firefighter thing."

"Well…… that's a bit of a thing right now," Fernando said.

"The firefighter said he paid the cost for the night at the Salem Inn. But, earlier today, the Innkeeper ran by our house…. I don't even know how he got our address…….and said that the night at the Salem Inn was never paid," William said.

"That's bad. I'll deal with that right now over the phone with the hotel and bank. Hmm. That's weird," Mr. Lowell said.

"What happened?" William asked.

"The phone line is down for the Salem Inn,"

"How about the bank?" Fernando asked.

"I'll try that now," Mr. Lowell said, pressing a button on his phone.

The phone beeped, indicating it automatically hung up on him.

"Oh great," Mr. Lowell said, rolling his eyes, frustrated, the phone lines wouldn't work.

"There must be a kink in the system," I said, stirring my pot of boiling ravioli round and round, creating a whirlpool in the center.

"Indeed. Could I please borrow your family car, Aspen?" Mr. Lowell asked.

"Certainly. After dinner. Your boys have missed you."

"We have," William said.

"Tell us all about your trip," Fernando said.

"Oh boy. It was crazy busy. I had a meeting every day and after our meetings, we tried a new restaurant every night. The first night was a seafood place. Then, we went to a Mexican place. And then, we tried an Italian place. Then, I ate lunch at the Potbellies at the airport before coming home to see you lovely people," Mr. Lowell said.

"Dinner is ready. This is vegetable ravioli with tomato sauce on top, served with a side of naans and cooked broccoli. Enjoy," I said, bringing bowls over to the table.

"This is wonderful," Mr. Lowell said, "I love pasta."

"Thank you," I said, sitting down to eat. I blew on my first piece of ravioli before taking my first bite. It was an explosion of flavors, sweet, smoky and spicy.

"So, tell me about Halloween," Mr. Lowell said.

"That could take all night," Fernando said.

"Give me the SparkNotes version. I think it'll be interesting. I've heard bits and pieces over the phone but not quite the full story," Mr. Lowell said.

"So, on Halloween we went out trick-or-treating, and a storm was rolling in that night. We walked down Essex Street and by the Ropes Mansion. The Ropes Mansion had a few windows lit as we walked by. We knew we needed to be home by ten on moms' orders," William started.

"However, as the weather conditions began to get worse, we lost cell reception and had to wait out the storm under an awning near a couple restaurants. I think we were next to Rockafellas and Gulu Gulu cafe. When the storm finally subsided, we headed together towards our house," Fernando added.

"Mom made us brownies, and we played some games. Mind you, by now we were all soaking wet and cold, so we changed. Aspen texted her parents for permission to stay with us until the storm was done, and we got a second wave of the storm, even worse than the first," William said, taking a bite of ravioli.

"Mom went upstairs, and as we were enjoying or trying to enjoy our dessert, we heard a crash, thud, and boom from upstairs. We smelled smoke and ran upstairs to find mom gone and a pink, puffy dress on fire in the hearth," Fernando said.

"How was this fire started?" Mr. Lowell asked.

"I don't know. We didn't start it. If anything, Mom would have," Fernando said.

"Or……. could it have been a ghost?" I asked.

Just at the mere suggestion that it could have been a ghost, Mr.

Lowell laughed. Just then, the wooden door that led out to the deck blew open slightly, creaking on its hinges, only to be slammed shut again.

"Who's there?" Mr. Lowell said.

No answer. Mr. Lowell shuttered.

"I don't believe in ghosts," Mr. Lowell said.

Another small creek sounded from somewhere farther away in the house. Goosebumps prickled up my spine.

"Well……. I guess I'd better be on my way to the Salem Inn soon as the clock is ticking," Mr. Lowell said, "I've decided I'm going to walk to clear my head. Aspen, thank you for letting us stay here with you until we find somewhere more permanent to live."

"No problem. Be safe out there Mr. Lowell."

"Bye. Safe travels. Love you Dad," William and Fernando said, each giving their dad a hug.

"Love you too. See you in the morning."

•

After Mr. Lowell had left out the front door with cash in hand to pay the manager at the hotel, we began to clean up the kitchen. We scrubbed all the bowls, put them in the dishwasher and ran it. The stars began to come out and the full moon made its appearance in the sky. Through the slightly cracked window it heard an owl hooting in the distance.

"You know what?" I said as we headed back upstairs.

"What?" Fernando asked.

"I think we should head out sooner rather than later," I said, then stopped at the top of the stairs to listen.

Fernando and William stopped behind me.

"Why'd you stop?" Fernando asked.

"Listen," I said.

A creaking was heard on the floorboards on the stairs. A heavy boot seemed to step, then step, and then drag across the floor. The jangle of the dishes in the cupboard indicated where the sounds were coming from. A shatter sounded from the kitchen with the same boots we heard before just faster as if running away from whatever it broke.

Then, there was silence except for the faucet running in the bathroom upstairs.

"Look," I said, pointing to the sink which had been left on for who knows how long.

"We need to get out of here. I'll turn it off," William said.

Church bells sounded in the distance. I began to count them. Four. Five. Six. Seven. Eight. Nine. Silence.

"I need to check the book before we go," I said.

"Make it quick," William said, fighting a yawn.

"Let's get you some coffee," Fernando said, "You look like you're about ready to fall asleep,"

"Sure," William said, shrugging tiredly.

I headed into my bedroom to find my book open on my bed glowing. It was not where I had left it before Mr. Lowell had arrived, which left me with all sorts of questions. Mr. Lowell was never up here, and neither were Fernando or William. The whisper of my own words earlier hovered over me. *What if it was a ghost?* Page 232 was open and seemed to be glowing red, then white, then bright orange, then yellow. When I tried to touch it, to read what the book had to say, it was hot to the touch.

My bedroom door creaked further open and slammed shut.

"William and Fernando. This is very funny!" I said.

No answer. The pipes started to creak again as I heard the water turn back on. I saw a flood of water start to trickle its way into my room.

The door clicked, indicating it was locked all on its own. The windows were frozen shut.

"William. Fernando. I need help!" I screamed, my heart racing.

The sound of the boots was in my room.

I took a deep breath and hummed the only thing that came to mind: Brahms Lullaby, a song my grandma used to hum to me growing up to get me to sleep while rubbing my back. It took everything inside me to calm down and not focus on the commotion going on around me. The book began to flash blue and became cool enough for just an instant for me to take a picture of the scribbled message on page 232. I promised myself I would read it later.

When I tried to lift the book off my bed, it didn't budge, just like the pocket watch. The book flashed red, orange, then yellow again, and I pulled my hand away, repelled by the intensity of the heat on my fingertips.

Stomp. Stomp. Stomp.

Tick. Tick. Tick.

"William. Fernando. Where are you?" I yelled.

No answer.

The shadow of a sailor began to appear on the floor. They had a three-pointed sailor hat, pointed boots, and a silhouette of a large overcoat. The shadow seemed to wave at me. An icy breeze blew across my ear. I ran towards the door and pulled the knob until it froze too. I grabbed my phone and turned on my flashlight to see if I could see this mystical being that seemed to be lurking in my room.

I shone my flashlight up and down, turned it sideways, until just for an instant like a flash of lightning I saw icy, almost beach wave blue eyes which appeared, then disappeared again. The stomping in my room grew louder. The stomping was towards me, cornering me towards a wall.

"How may I help you?" I asked, this being that seemed to be lurking in my bedroom. I was hyper aware of my pulse that seemed to be racing with every step back from the being I took until my back met the wall. My hand on the wall felt as if it was on a warm, human chest as if it rose and fell. Up. down. In. Out. The steady beat of a pulse seemed to thrum underneath my other hand. I heard ocean waves faintly in the distance, as I closed my eyes, I pictured them. I saw the waves licking the shore at night as the water shone under the moonlight.

The waves weren't the only thing I saw though, rather there was a boat bobbing some distance out from the shore with a skull and crossbones sail. This boat had a lantern on the starboard side and the flame within the lantern bobbed as the waves hit the boat again and again. Within the sea breeze as snow begins to fall, I hear the whisper, "I need to be free from the sea," The whisper has a lisp and is raspy and low. I open my eyes transfixed by the sound around me. *Thurm. Thrum. Stomp. Stomp. Drag. Silence.*

The door clicks, creaks open, slams shut once again, the key turning in the lock. *Stomp. Stomp. Whoosh. Silence.*

"William. Fernando. Can you let me out?" I said, pounding on the door.

"Aspen?" Fernando said.

"I'm in my room," I called, "We need to get out of here before the clock strikes midnight."

"Where's the key?" Fernando asked.

"Good question. I don't know," I said, "One sec."

My hand hovered over the book that glowed yellow, red, then orange, then went black. *The answer is inside.* I closed my eyes and thought of keys. The book was frigid with a mist lingering over it

ASPEN

I was four years old, lying in bed, looking up at my ceiling. The sheep went round and round, my sound spa playing ocean waves that were meant to be soothing. No matter how hard I tried, I couldn't fall asleep. I wasn't tired at all. So, I got up and wandered downstairs. My light footsteps on the stairs weren't heard by my parents as I continued to tiptoe down the stairs. The door to the family room was closed yet not locked. I pressed my eye into the keyhole to watch the adults in the room.

"When do we tell the kids about our family history?" Mom was saying to Dad. They had the radio playing in the background and a few lamps turned on.

"They'll get flashes," Dad said.

"Should we leave hints for them?"

"They're smart. They can figure it out,"

Mr. Lowell stood up to pour himself another glass of eggnog.

Why are the Lowell's there?

Mrs. Lowell stood up as well and added a log to the fire in the fireplace. Above the hearth read, "Warmest wishes,"

A cauldron of some sort of cider heated over the fire.

I smelled cinnamon, clove, and apple through the keyhole.

"I'm going to get our glasses from the kitchen," Mom said.

I tried to scurry away quietly, but unsuccessfully.

"Why are you still awake, darling?" Mom asked, seeing me as I tried to scamper away.

"Couldn't sleep," I said.

In the dim light, I squint and see a golden chain on my mom's neck. Whatever is at the end of it is tucked into her red and green sweater.

Doesn't grandma have the same necklace?

SEARCHING FOR WILLIAM

A tap on my shoulder caused me to jump.

"Hi there!" Fernando said.

"How did you get in here?" I asked.

"I picked the lock," Fernando said, showing me a bobby pin.

"How smart! Great job! Where's William?" I asked.

"He closed his eyes for a little bit, then had a bad dream again and woke up. You know how it goes."

"Let's go find him," I said.

"He's in our guest bedroom," Fernando said.

"We walked toward the guest bedroom to find the door open, with no one inside,"

"I swear, he was," Fernando said.

"I believe you."

"Look," Fernando pointed at the open front door.

"Oh. Great," I said.

A silence hung over us as we thought about what to do next.

"He must have escaped. You were sure he was awake, right? Not just sleep talking?"

"It's entirely possible he could have been sleep talking," Fernando said, "Sometimes, according to our parents, we actually have conversations while we're sleeping,"

"Interesting. We'd better head out. I have a feeling I know exactly where William is going. I'm going to try to grab the book one more time,"

I headed back into my bedroom and tried to lift the non-glowing book from my bed. It still didn't budge. Neither did the pocket watch.

"What was the crash in the kitchen I heard earlier?" I asked.

"It was a pint glass breaking. I didn't break it. I think whatever was here earlier broke the pint glass,"

Or whoever.

"Let's clean it up when we get back."

Fernando and I headed out into the night. I inhaled the crisp, cold night air, and let my feet guide me. I had my mini cauldron in hand and walked briskly with Fernando on my heels. He held his flashlight, and the light swayed back and forth as we walked. We took a right at the end of the street and then followed the street all the way down to Ropes Mansion and then took a left.

"Look," I said, pointing down at the sidewalk.

Muddy footprints zigzagged across the sidewalk. We followed them and eventually, we found ourselves in the woods in the middle of the night. I knew the woods we were inside of. I began to recognize the tree roots and stones along the path we walked. We walked up switchback after switchback until we reached the top of the mountain and found grandma's house. The footprints continued up the porch steps and into the house.

I looked at the door knocker. The doorknocker's eyes were open and seemed to be going around in circles. Bright, neon green light reflected on the doorknocker's face, and the ring hung in the doorknocker's mouth seemed to be hanging on by a crooked tooth. Beneath the first face on the door, was another face, which I immediately recognized, and my pulse quickened.

"William," I said, my face scrunching up in anger.

His face in the door didn't have a ring in his mouth yet. His eyes were closed peacefully as if dreaming.

I knocked on the door, next to my grandma's face. The door knocker jumped in surprise, and said, "Oh. Hi Aspen. Just one moment."

There was rummaging around in the house and then what sounded like a large piece of furniture was being moved. Then a nearby click sounded.

"Come on in," Grandma said, opening the door.

"Thank you. We're looking for William," I said.

"He's sleeping in the guest room. Gave him stardust," Grandma said.

"Oh. How peaceful is his sleep?" I asked.

"Not peaceful at all. He keeps on twitching," she said, stirring a black curved pot on the stove, glowing neon green.

"What are you making?" Fernando asked.

"Nothing."

"Can I see William?" I asked.

"No. He needs more rest," Grandma said.

I set my miniature cauldron down on the table near the door and stepped inside my grandma's cottage. She grew plants on the windowsill. They were labeled: "Timely Thyme" "Sparkly Sage" "Beauty Basil" "Dimple Dill" "Outstanding Oregano"

Thyme to think about time.

"Grandma."

"Yes dear?"

"Have you ever had a pocket watch?"

"Never."

"Do you mind if we borrow some of your thyme?" I asked.

"Not at all. Let me finish my pot…um……. Er……. concoction in this pot."

"I knew you were making a potion! What does it do?" I asked.

"It shows us what is going on in Williams' head," Grandma answered.

"Because he won't talk about his dreams," I said.

"That's so smart," Fernando said.

"The only problem is that it's fragmented. Watch," Grandma said.

He's walking towards the Ropes Mansion. The sky seems to linger above him as he walks, heavy step after heavy step until he meets an older man in the street walking towards him in the opposite direction. He meets Willliam halfway. No words are exchanged between the two of them. They just look at each other. William seems to be searching for something.

The older man is someone I recognize. He has a long white beard, is short and has glasses. He seems to be peering over his glasses at William. I closed my eyes for a second and thought of where I'd seen him before. The Salem Inn. *I continued to watch as the older man pulled his key ring out of his right pocket of his khaki shorts. One of the keys was identical to the key I had seen in my dream. Gold, long and shiny. It shimmered in a stray ray of sunlight. He jingled the keys a few times as he flipped from one key to the next. He finally found the car key he was looking for and pressed the button to unlock the car. It beeped.*

The man climbed into his car and drove away as William continued to walk along the street and towards the Ropes Mansion. He ran his fingers along the railing and walked up the stairs one by one by one. His hand goes to the doorknob which doesn't budge. William tries to shake it open; it still doesn't budge.

His eyes go up to look at the top right window, the only one lit in the house. A silhouette is pacing in the room while William watches. Then, the amber light seems to take over the entire house and a loud ringing sound. Blackness takes over the neon green potion and the ringing stops. Salt droplets emerge from the potion.

"He's awake," Grandma said.

"I'm going up there to make sure he's okay," Fernando said.

"Okay."

Fernando heads upstairs, and I pull out my phone to show Grandma the picture of the recipe I received in the book.

"Oh boy! I'm so happy for you!" Grandma said.

"Thanks! I'm hoping it's okay if I use your kitchen to make this recipe."

"Thyme to think about time.
If it isn't too late
Be sure you ate
Enough so you don't debate
Future generations' fate.
The past is something we can recreate
As we wait" I read aloud.

"I love that poem. Does it come with the recipe?" Grandma asked.

"Yes."

The recipe read:

Note: Must be made in a cauldron.

Miso Potato Soup

Ingredients:
1 cup miso paste
4 sprigs timely thyme
2 handfuls russet potatoes
3 cups water (from a nearby well)
1 tablespoon salt (derived from sweat)
1 tablespoon olive oil

1) Stir miso, water and salt in a warm cauldron until boiling, and steaming.
2) Add potatoes to the miso mixture and stir for 20 minutes until potatoes have softened entirely.
3) Add timely thyme, cover and swirl a few times. Let sit for at least 10 minutes before consumption.
4) Drizzle with olive oil and eat warm.

The hot cauldron of midnight miso soup was flavorful and rich. I headed upstairs to get William and Fernando to try my soup. They came bounding down the stairs. William still looked awfully tired as we ate. Every time we took a bite, I thought of a boy version of him, barely awake enough to not fall asleep in his cereal bowl. I smiled coyly all throughout dinner.

As we continued to eat, the droplets hovering over the potion swirled around to make the shape of a key. The more soup we ate, the more solid the key became. It shone in the moonlight streaming in through the window over the kitchen sink. It was intricately made with each and every detail intended into it with every bite of soup we ate. Golden strands of magic seemed to create a cage of sorts around the key as it was made. The large cauldron underneath it began to cool off and the neon green liquid turned into crystal clear crystals. Upon finishing our last bites of stew, the key dropped onto the crystal bed and rested there.

"Go forth with this key, unlock the past, and be careful," Grandma said, picking the key up from its resting spot and handing it to me.

"Time is precious," I said, holding out my hand for the key.

"Savor every second you have to change and grow. You will never get a moment back from the past unless you change it. My hope lies with your generation," Grandma said.

My brain tried desperately to interpret those words but came up empty. *Change the past? I thought the past was what it was for a reason. Everything has a purpose, yet here I'm being told to change what has happened. Why?*

I turned the golden key over in my hand as the first rays of sunlight after the long night crept in through the window. It sparkled in the sunlight.

"Hide the key, keep it safe. Don't let it fall into the wrong hands. If it does, you'll have consequences," Grandma warned.

"I will keep it safe," I said.

Fernando and William watched in bemusement as Grandma, and I exchanged goodbyes. The plethora of wisdom I had gained from her was something I was so grateful for, and I loved her more for it.

"Congratulations on everything you did tonight."

"Thank you."

"I love you, Aspen dear," Grandma said, pulling me in for a hug.

"Love you too," I said, giving her a nice long squeeze.

"Now, go discover what your key has to unlock," Grandma said.

•

William and Fernando followed me as we headed out into the chilly, crisp morning air. We hightailed it back home at a brisk pace, but every step of the way, Angus, the crow, seemed to be following us. I carried my miniature cauldron on my left arm and walked down the path until Angus dropped a scroll of parchment paper in front of us, just before we left the woods. It read: *Stardust story is captured within the book. Will be shown to you at the moment when you most need it.* I recognized the cursive immediately. It was so familiar.

"Thank you, Grandma," I whispered.

"That was surely interesting," Fernando said.

"Agreed," William said.

William, for the first time in a few days, seemed more upbeat and awake than he had in the past few days.

"I'm so glad we went," I said.

"How did we get to your grandma's house in the first place?" William asked.

"Well…… you were dreaming," Fernando said, "And…,"

"Oh," William said, putting two and two together, "But why would I walk to your grandma's house during a dream?"

"I don't know. I think it has something to do with your subconscious. Something you know deep down but, on the surface, you haven't faced yet," I said.

We had reached the sidewalk by now and headed toward my house as we watched the yellow leaves fall in the breeze. The yellow and orange clouds as the sun rose over the horizon were pretty. They left me awestruck as we kept on walking. The trees added to the scenery as black silhouettes, slowly being illuminated by the gradually rising sun.

"Dad should be home by the time we get there," William said.

"Yes, he should be. I hope the manager wasn't irritated about the later payment than they're used to," Fernando added.

As we made the last few turns to arrive at my house, I remembered my responsibilities for Pluto. He would need to be taken outside and fed when I got home. Then, another thing occurred to me. How come Pluto never sensed the spirits in our house last night? Maybe animals don't pick up on the same sounds and signals humans do?

When we arrived home, opened the garage, and headed inside, the house was eerily quiet.

"Dad," Fernando called.

"Dad,"

No answer.

I took Pluto outside, checking the backyard for Mr. Lowell. He was nowhere to be found. I went back inside to feed Pluto and talk to William and Fernando.

"Dads missing now too? Oh great," William said, sarcastically as he paced back and forth in the kitchen anxiously.

"Careful. The pint glass broke in the kitchen," I said.

"Right. Whoops," William said, side stepping away from where it broke.

"We need to trust our dad can take care of himself," Fernando said.

"And how do you think we do that?" William said, running his fingers through his hair.

"We just have to let go," Fernando said.

"And besides, we have a brand-new, custom-made key right here and two locks in this house. I think the key to finding your mom and Dad is to unlock whatever this is the key is to," I said.

"Her grandma did say something about a better future from a resolved past," Fernando said.

"You're right," William said, "Okay, I guess I'm in on trying the key on the locks. Under one condition though,"

"What is your condition?" I asked.

"I need a peaceful night of sleep. No dreams, no nightmares, no sleepwalking, no sleep talking, no nothing. Just sleep," William said.

"Deal," I said.

I scribbled away on a piece of parchment paper. It read:
Peaceful, Dreamless Night Stardust Requested ASAP. Love you! Aspen.

"Angus," I called out the kitchen window.

The crow that had followed us home came back, took the parchment paper from my hand and flew away.

"You can communicate with crows?" Fernando asked.

"Yes. Pretty cool right?" I asked.

"Yes,"

"Let's go test my key on the closet items," I said, "We only have a matter of chimes,"

"Funny," Fernando said.

"No really, it's time sensitive. We don't have all day," I said.

We headed upstairs and went into Fernando and Williams guest room first because I suspected my key would open the pocket watch sitting on the table near the miniature tree in their closet. I held the heart lock in my hand and turned the key to hear a click.

"We're in," I said.

The pocket watch opened to reveal the time and a purple ring around the outside of the watch seemed to go round and round until it turned gold and the hands of the clock started to move as well. Then the whole clock went white and stretched larger and larger. Golden strands of magic pulled us by our flailing arms, legs, and torsos into a different world. A world that would change all of us - forever.

MR. LOWELL

Twelve Hours Before

As I walked, there was a lingering dread and worry hanging over me. I never have liked it when payments never went through and required you to go pay in person. I knew I needed to continue walking and make sure the night got paid off. I hoped everything would turn out fine and I'd be on my way back to Aspen's house by nine.

I walked by the Ropes Mansion at sunset, the back half was illuminated by sunlight, while the front half was completely dark. No windows illuminated. I kept walking past the Ropes Mansion, down another street, and the chill in the air only grew as I walked. Eventually, after a few more turns, I reached the Salem Inn.

With the cash in my pocket, I walked up the stairs to the main red brick building, opened the heavy door and walked into the lobby area.

"Good evening," The older man behind the desk said. He was short with a white beard and spectacles. He wore a black bathrobe and a nightcap. That struck me as strange. Usually, hotel managers had a uniform to wear, but this man didn't seem to have a uniform whatsoever. It was fine for him to wear his pajamas to work.

"I wanted to pay for a night at the Salem Inn about three nights ago. My sons and their friend stayed here,"

"Ahhhh. I see,"

"I brought you some cash," I said, showing the manager.

"I'll take that," he said, taking the stack of bills from my hand and counting each one.

"You're twenty dollars short," He informed me. I sighed in frustration.

"Oh, well I'd better be going back home to retrieve the rest of the cash for you. Do you take credit cards?" I asked.

"No. I can tell you're tired. Why don't you stay here for a night?" He asked.

"What about the twenty-four-hour deadline?" I asked.

"You can pay the rest in the morning," He replied.

Sensing this was some sort of trick, I said, "I'd rather go home and come back with the rest of the cash in the morning to save money,"

"Are you sure about that?" He asked.

The door opened and clicked shut behind me as another guest came in. The next guest waited to check in behind me.

"Yes. I'd better be going now," I said.

Something about the front desk manager didn't seem quite right.

"Not so fast…," The manager seemed to mutter as the next guest stepped up.

I pulled on the heavy door. It didn't budge. I pushed the heavy door; it still didn't budge. I looked at the brass lock on the door. It was turned all the way to the right, indicating it was locked. The grandfather clock behind the hotel manager's desk chimed on the hour. Nine o'clock at night. I tried to turn the lock, but it wouldn't budge.

After every vibration of the chime had been silenced, I was hyper aware that I was being watched. Both the new guest and the hotel manager had paused their conversation to watch me struggle to open the heavy door. The hotel manager had a smug expression on his face as he watched me.

"Let me help you," said the new guest, checking in. His jaw twitched slightly to the right as he pulled as hard as he could on the door. He tried to unlock it, just as I had. It wouldn't budge. It was as if heavy metal was stuck in place.

"I don't think it'll open. Maybe it needs some oil?" he said, shrugging.

Tick. Tick. Tick.

"Sir. You wanted one room. Is that correct?" The hotel manager asked.

"Yes. On the East side, if possible,"

"Yes, it most certainly is. You'll be in the East Peabody house room number twelve. Here's your room key. Happy hauntings,"

"Thanks," He said, nodding to the hotel manager, and taking a seat in the lobby.

From his left breast pocket of his overcoat, he pulled a golden pocket watch out and opened it, watching the hands as they kept on ticking.

I stepped up to the counter again and said, "It appears as though I can't leave. Can you unlock the doors please?"

"No, we're closed to new guests on Sundays at nine pm. No one is allowed to come in or out," The manager said.

"My family is on their way into town right now. I just checked in for them, and you're saying that they can't get in now?" The other guest said.

"Rules are rules," The manager said.

"I guess I'd better book an alternative hotel for my family as I'm stuck here for the night," The guest said.

"I guess I'd like a room," I said, begrudgingly.

"You're in room seventeen East, Mr. Lowell. Happy Hauntings," The manager said, handing me a hotel key.

"I know exactly where that is," The other guest said, "I can show you to your room if you'd like,"

"That would be great," I said.

"I'll have the toiletry essentials delivered within the hour," The hotel manager said.

"Okay," I said, irritated. I'd never planned for a night at the Salem Inn, and another night to pay for on top of the rest of my expenses. I followed the other man down the candle lit hallway. He pulled his luggage behind him and wore a crossbody duffle bag.

"I never introduced myself. My apologies. I'm Mr. Chimes," he said, giving me a firm handshake.

"Pleasure to meet you," I said, "I'm Mr. Lowell,"

"Nice to meet you too,"

"First night here?" he asked, nose twitching.

"Yes," I said, nodding.

"Well let's just say that this is a spooky place close to Halloween time. Strange things happen at night here," he said quietly as we turned left at the end of the hallway.

The floorboards creaked underneath our feet. I thought I heard a faint purring sound, and a couple light footsteps but I couldn't be sure.

Mr. Chimes' pocket watch continued to tick, as we walked down yet another hallway and finally arrived at room seventeen East. I met his eyes in the dim light of the hallway, and they went wide as a purple glow came from the pocket watch. The light shone through the fabric of his flannel shirt.

"Oh boy," he said, trying to cover up the light. The ticking grew faster.

"Good night Mr. Lowell," Mr. Chimes said.

"Good night. Thanks for walking me to my room," I said.

"I'd better be going now," he said, as his pocket watch let out a sound that I could only describe as a half screech, and half ringing sound.

I pulled my room key out of my pocket, inserted it in the lock and it clicked indicating I was in the room. I closed the door behind me, turned on some lights and immediately walked over to the kitchenette. On the kitchenette counter sat a basket of assorted snacks and water bottles. I immediately grabbed the bag of freshly salted, still warm popcorn off the counter and grabbed the remote to turn the TV on.

After clicking through all the channels, I finally found a movie to watch for a bit until my essential toiletries arrived. About ten minutes into watching *Ghostbusters*. I heard a knock at the door, slowly climbed out of bed and opened the door to find a stack of towels and a plastic bag with all the essential travel toiletries I could possibly need inside of it. When I picked up the bag, there was a circular piece of parchment paper tied to it with twine. I untied the twine and read the note attached. It read:

Meet me at breakfast tomorrow morning in the lobby. Don't be late.

Underneath the message was a picture of a clock. The hour hand pointed at nine and the minute hand pointed at 12.

"Nine in the morning," I muttered to myself. I immediately knew from the last sentence who this message was from: Mr. Chimes.

I continued to watch TV and eat my popcorn until the TV channel started flipping back and forth between freeform, where *Ghostbusters* was on and the nightly news. My hands did nothing with the remote. *Maybe the TV has a glitch.* I decided to turn the TV off, shower and get ready for bed. As I showered, the pipes in the walls around me seemed to creak and moan. The water was pleasantly warm at first, but quickly turned icy cold before I was done, causing me to let out a yelp. I tried to mess with the temperature of the water to turn it back to warm again, but the water only got colder.

Eventually, I gave up and told myself I'd shower at Aspen's house in the morning. I got dressed in the same clothes I'd worn here, and climbed into the bed, which felt as hard as a rock. I turned the overhead light off, locked the door, and tried to close my eyes and rest. The pounding of my heart and my rapid breathing were the only things I heard as sleep drew nearer and nearer. My heart slowed, and my breath slowed.

Stomp. Stomp.

I opened my eyes and listened. The stomping continued. It seemed to be coming from the hallway outside my room. A scratch sounded outside my door as the lock on my door clicked open all by itself. A chilly breeze blew into my room, and I was wide awake. The door opened an inch at first, then another inch and continued to open slowly but surely. The hinges let out a loud screech as the door opened all the way. Then, the door slammed shut.

Chills ran down my spine. Somebody or something was in my room.

Knock! Knock! Knock!

Just then, the closet door creaked open and immediately closed.

I climbed out of bed trembling in fear, my palms sweaty to open the door. On the other side of the door stood a man with a brown beard, a nightcap, and glasses.

"I'm Mr. Higginbottom's. I can hear you stomping from all the way down the hall and I'd like some rest," he said, irritated.

I nodded. He walked back to his room at the end of the hall and the door swung closed. In the darkness of my room, I padded my way back to my bed, crawled in and pulled the covers up to my shoulders. *There are no ghosts here.*

As if someone was listening to my thoughts and trying to prove me wrong, a stomp sounded in the closet, followed by another stomp and a huge ear shattering thud. I opened the closet door to see what had broken. In pieces on the closet floor was a bottle that long ago would have carried rum in a ship.

I instantly dialed the number left on my bedside table for housekeeping to come clean up the broken rum bottle. Inside the closet there was nothing outside the ordinary upon first glance. There was an ironing table, a suitcase stand, a few hangers and further back in the corner was the broken rum glass. Next to the rum glass was another half full rum glass and a wet spot on the carpet in the back left corner. The chilly breeze tickled my neck, and the sheets began to move towards the bottom of the bed as if they were about to be taken off the bed to be washed.

Knock. Knock. Knock.

At first, I thought the housekeeping people would be here to clean up the mess. Instead, I opened the door to reveal Mr. Higginbottom's. He uttered no other words than, "Shhhhhhhh" and walked away.

Stomp. Stomp. Stomp. Stomp.

Four heavy footsteps sounded, right next to the four-poster bed and the mattress sagged under the weight of something I was unable to see. *I must be imagining this. I swear I'm dreaming.* I blinked as if it would make what I saw in the dim lighting of my room go away. Everything was the same as before I had blinked. If not the same, then slightly spookier. The faucet handle began to turn on all by itself, starting the flow of water in the sink.

Knock. Knock.

"Housekeeping," A man said outside the door.

"Coming," I said, trying to turn the faucet handle off, and being unsuccessful. It was as if the same metal the door was made of was on the faucet handles too, causing them to refuse to budge. The sink started to overflow as I ran towards the door to let housekeeping in.

"What seems to be the problem?" The man asked. He held a vacuum in one hand and a broom and dustpan in the other.

"Everything," I wanted to scream. Instead, I took a breath and said, "The faucet won't turn off. There's a broken rum bottle in the closet and a huge wet spot in the back left of the closet,"

As the housekeeper tried to clean up the broken rum bottle, the broom kept trying to leave his grasp until the *thing* pulling it from the other end succeeded and used the end of the broom to bonk the housekeeper on the head. I watched in horrified shock as the housekeeper fell to the ground and the door to my hotel room slammed shut once again. As the door slammed shut, I saw Mr. Higginbottom's in the doorframe, his pointer finger pressed to his lips saying, "Shhh,"

I felt an icy breeze prickle up my back and down my arms. I listened to the sounds around me as the chill lingered in the air. The pipes seemed to quiet down, and the faucet handles turned themselves in the opposite direction as before. The water only dripped from the facet now. The breeze seemed to whoosh in a different direction this time. The closet door creaked open again and this time a hatbox, decorated with ribbon and lace, floated in midair. I could only see this from the moonlight streaming in through the window. The box was placed down on the desk, and the quill floated in midair, making a few brushstrokes on the parchment paper that waited for ink. I walked over to read the message left on the piece of parchment.

Sit. Look. Read. Feel.

I sat down to stare at the hatbox. The mattress creaked once again, causing me to jump. Whatever *thing* was in this room with me was sitting on the edge of the bed. I felt as though I was being watched. I took a deep breath and whispered, "I do not believe in ghosts,"

An icy breeze hovered over my right ear. On the breeze I heard the words, "We're real," I smelled the faint scent of salt for just an instant and then it was gone. My heart thumped in my chest as I sat down at the desk and opened the box. I clicked the button to turn the lamp on adjacent to the desk. The amber lighting that filled the room was on for just an instant and almost immediately turned back off. The quill hovered in midair again, dipped itself into ink and in sweeping strokes wrote on the parchment once again.

Light not needed. You'll see.

The quill floated back over to the ink jar, put itself back in place and the icy breeze seemed to hover over me for some time until I finally exhaled, and gave in to my curiosity. I opened the box, peered inside, and found a pair of blue tinted spectacles. At first all the pages inside the box seemed meaningless and blank. I rummaged through the box to find different types of ribbon, string, twine, etc. that tied each piece of paper together. The first one on top was tied with twine and entirely blank on the front and back.

Stomp! Stomp!

"Be patient," I said, into thin air. Then, I immediately covered my mouth. *Am I talking to ghosts now?*

I looked back at the four words on the parchment paper. *Sit. Look. Read. Feel.*

I grabbed the spectacles that sat on top of the stack of letters and peered through them. Everything around me transformed to look entirely different than before. I gasped at the ocean blue eyes that seemed to be staring at me from the other side of the desk. A whole transparent figure hovered over the desk just staring. She had icy blue skin, perfect ringlets, and a crisp, white gown on. I couldn't believe my eyes. *This can't be happening.*

I took the glasses back off and the icy breeze immediately hovered over my right shoulder, "Believe," the breeze said. I took a deep, shaky breath and put the spectacles back on, trying my best to slow down my racing heart. I saw the ghostly woman floating over to the bed, perching on the edge, waiting for me to discover what she's been waiting for me to find all night. I couldn't believe I was listening to this whisper in the breeze and putting the spectacles back on. Something deep inside me prodded me further. I was just as curious as this *being* that I started to feel a bond. Was it a family bond? A friendship bond? Something deeper? I could never be sure. I knew there was a spark there. I knew that there was a reason why I was here at this time.

Read. I unrolled the first piece of parchment, pushed the glasses up on the bridge of my nose and began to read:

December 1st, 1804

Dearest Nate,

I haven't got a clue where to start with this letter, so I thought I'd start from the beginning and tell you why I'm writing. I miss you, so I thought writing to you would help me feel as if you're here with me. To an extent, it does. I can feel you in this room with me perhaps scribbling away on a notepad or sticking your nose in your next new favorite book. But now I can't help but wonder what you're doing right now. I know you're on a ship headed towards the Mediterranean. I could imagine you with both hands on the wheel as the waves rock the boat and the wind blows in the sails. I wonder who you've met on your trip so far and await the day you arrive home and tell me all about it.

Best wishes, pirate!
Katherine

How did this start? I wondered. *How long has Nate been at sea at this point and when does he return home?*

The faucet handle began to creak again, and I looked up to see the blue ghostly figure plugging the drain. I squint at her, and her blue lips say a silent word to me. I caught it the first time. *Feel.* The pipes began to creak and moan again on the hallway side of the room. I touch a fingertip to the wall first and then two. The water keeps running and as it does, I take the glasses off and close my eyes. Back to the wall, my feet are frozen in place.

Warmth floods my fingertips and then I begin to feel a pulse underneath my hand that isn't my own. Underneath my other hand the wall rises and falls as if my hand were on a human's chest. Behind my eyes is pure blackness until I hear a seagull flapping in the distance and feel a cold, salty ocean breeze on my skin. A brunette woman with perfect ringlets framing her face stared out at the sea longingly on top of a white mansion.

Tick. Tick. Tick. With each tick of time, her position changed from standing to sitting to reading to writing to sleeping to looking through binoculars, just waiting. Her posture grew more anxious as time went by. She would grow fidgety and anxious, grow strained, and her face became blotchy as she waited. Somewhere deep inside, I knew she was waiting for Nate to arrive home. Yet, there was never any joy in him arriving home, which worried me.

CRACK! I was jolted by the vision, as I rushed to the bathroom. The room had begun to flood. The pipe underneath the sink had cracked and water was spewing everywhere.

I called room service for the second time that night. Before they arrived, I hid the letters on the uppermost shelf in the closet. Three brisk knocks came at the door.

"Housekeeping,"

I opened the door to find a new butler.

"I'm so sorry to wake you. I promise I never did any of this. It was all the spirits you have lingering at your hotel,"

"No worries, Sir. Believe me, we have seen and heard much worse. Everything always happens at night. That's why we take night shifts. Every shift never gets boring,"

I nodded.

"I'll have you vacate your room for about an hour or so until we have your room cleaned and dried in addition to the pipe repaired. No cost on your part," The butler said.

"Thank you," I said and briskly walked to the lobby.

I must have walked the wrong way at first because a very tired, frustrated Mr. Higginbottoms poked his head out of his room to "*shhhhhhh*" me another time. I turned around and walked the other way more slowly and mindfully this time focusing on landing lightly on my toes. As I walked down the dimly lit hallway, the floorboards creaked underneath my feet and a black cat meowed in the distance. I kept walking as this night just seemed to get spookier. I blinked and reopened my eyes to spot a white fluffball hopping down the hallway.

I rubbed my eyes, convinced that I was hallucinating from the lack of sleep. I reopened my eyes, and the rabbit was still there hopping up the right side of the hallway and stopping every few hops to inspect something. The rabbit seemed to jingle with every hop. He carried something with him. All I could see from the dim light was the golden chain it hung on.

I tried to get closer and closer without scaring the rabbit.

"1990. No," Someone muttered, "Too soon,"

"1993. No, wrong year," the same voice muttered again. The voice sounded vaguely familiar. The bunny kept hopping and stopped again to look at the numbers on little doors along the wall that I hadn't noticed before. Each door had a year written on it. I tiptoed closer to the bunny, and it turned and jumped back in surprise. As it jumped, I saw the golden pocket watch in the right breast pocket of his bunny shaped overcoat.

"2000," The rabbit said, reading the numbers on the door he was next to.

"Just right. Better be going. Mustn't be late," The same voice said again.

Ding. Ding. Rang the pocket watch as the bunny hopped through the door.

I must be dreaming right now.

I continued to walk through the hallway and down a flight of stairs to the lobby. It felt as though light footsteps padded down the stairs on my side mimicking my movement. At the bottom of the staircase there was a plaque that read: *Beware of the fourth step.* I continued on my way to the lobby, down another hallway and another until I saw the light of several lamps at the end. Not only were many lamps on, but the hotel manager was also down there sleeping and snoring in his chair at the front desk. *Did he ever leave that chair? Or have any time off?*

His snoring grew louder as I got closer. I sat down on a yellow couch just a few feet away from him which seemed to swallow me whole. I felt as though I was so low to the ground that I would have a hard time getting back up. So, I decided it might not be a bad idea to recline and close my eyes for a few minutes. It was light down here, so there would be no need to worry about ghosts floating around or anything.

I relaxed on the couch, and before I knew it, the soothingly loud snores of the hotel manager faded away and I was transported into dreamland.

I shivered, teeth chattering, snowflakes falling around me.

Some landed on the rails of a sailboat, some landed on my head, some zigzagged their way down in the icy breeze. I felt numb as I watched the flakes fall. Following a flake in the air, it drew my attention to a sailboat bobbing in the water. Ice sheets surrounded the boat. From the distance, I saw a skull and crossbones sail and a dimly lit lantern on the stern. The flame dipped and bobbed. Warmth.

I seemed to be floating in midair towards the flame to warm my fingertips and stop my jaw from shaking due to the chill in the air, and then the boat began to move, and I followed it until it disappeared in the fog. The fog was so deep that I couldn't even see the lantern glowing on the stern. The snow seemed thicker in the fog, and I became lost, searching for the light, and warmth I knew the boat would provide me until it faded into darkness.

I was being poked by someone.

"Sir. Sir," Someone was saying.

I woke up to find the hotel manager looking at me.

"Breakfast starts in ten minutes. I need you to head up to your room," The manager said, pointing towards the hallway that led to the stairs, a stern expression on his face.

"Is it clean?" I asked.

"I don't know," He replied.

"I'll go check," I said.

I walked up to my room to find the same butler from last night, still unconscious on the floor, and the other one vacuuming up the shards of glass from the rum bottle. A pillow floated in midair.

"Um. Sir. I dropped my keys on the floor," I said over the sound of the vacuum, urging him to bend over and pick them up.

He did, and the pillow just missed the back of his head, landing on the upper shelf of the closet by the hatbox. *Oh.* I never finished all the letters last night. There must be more I needed to discover. I looked down at my watch. *Oh shoot!* The time read 9:10.

"I'm going down to breakfast. Let me know when you're done," I shouted over the vacuum cleaner.

"Yes, sir!" The butler said.

I rushed down to the breakfast buffet in the lobby as fast as my feet would take me, arriving down at the lobby in about five minutes flat. I was walking so fast and not watching where I was going that I plowed right into Mr. Higginbottoms on my way down the hall.

"Watch where you're going!" He said, giving me an icy glare.

"My apologies," I called over my shoulder as I continued to walk towards the lobby.

"Sorry I'm late," I said, out of breath when I reached the lobby and joined Mr. Chimes at a table.

"No problem. Let's hop in line," he said, literally hopping into line. I laughed.

"How'd you sleep?" I asked.

"I'll let you in on a little secret: I never sleep here. Nobody does," he said, quietly.

A platter of pancakes and omelets came out from the kitchen and the scent wafted over to where we stood in line. Mr. Chimes' nose started twitching.

"Remind me which room you stayed in," I said.

"It was on the East side and let's just say it was freezing cold there all night. I'm actually glad my wife and children didn't stay here. They wouldn't have slept a wink," he said, laughing to himself.

"My wife gets rather cranky when she doesn't sleep," he said.

The color drained from my face, and I couldn't help but long to see my wife again. I closed my eyes for an instant and thought of her. Her laugh was always a deep belly laugh and throughout our marriage I had always tried to be witty, just to hear that laugh one more time. She and I loved to hike together all times of year and enjoy books together near a warm, comforting fire.

Mr. Chimes and I stepped up to the food buffet and filled our plates with anything we wanted. For the whole time we stood near the food buffet, Mr. Chimes' nose wouldn't stop twitching. He filled his plate with an egg omelet, banana, and arugula. He grabbed some packets of ketchup and some hash brown patties and continued walking to a table and sat down.

I filled my plate with two egg omelets, a bagel, and hash brown patties. Then, followed Mr. Chimes to a table and sat down.

"You look solemn," Mr. Chimes noted.

"My wife went missing recently and I miss her," I said.

"I see. I'm sorry to hear that," Mr. Chimes said, sympathetically.

"It's okay. It'll have to be okay until we find her," I said, "So tell me more about this place. I take it, this is not your first time here?"

He chewed his omelet thoughtfully before smiling, revealing an overbite of his front two teeth.

"This place around town gets a bad rap because of all the things that are said to have happened here and believe me, the list is long," Mr. Chimes said.

"I think I experienced some of that last night," I said.

"Maybe," He said, shrugging, "But there may be more to it than just whatever happened last night,"

"Like what?"

"This place dates back a long, long time and according to the stories that go around, some of the spirits of the people that lived here long ago still haunt the inn,"

"That's spooky,"

"Very true. What happened in your room last night?" Mr. Chimes said, raising a brow, "I've stayed in there before, and let's just say the night I was there was a night I'll never forget,"

I sighed. "Well.... for starters a fellow guest by the name of Mr. Higginbottoms......," I trailed off as Mr. Higginbottoms walked by our table to take a seat with a black haired, exhausted-looking woman, who cradled a baby in her arms.

I lowered my voice to a whisper, "He kept coming to my room and shushed me,"

"Did he really?" Mr. Chimes asked, seemingly knowing that it wasn't me he should have been shushing.

"Yes. But, the whole time, it wasn't me who was making a ruckus. I had to call room service twice last night, and I feel awful because the poor guys seem to have to workday and night like crazy," I said.

"I had to call them once last night because my thermostat wouldn't turn up and the balcony door wouldn't close," Mr. Chimes said, "Somehow the balcony door opened all by itself and by the time room service got up to my room and they tried to close the door, it slammed right in the butler's face which locked him out on the balcony. Then, the door locked all by itself, and the butler banged on the door trying to get back inside,"

"Did he ever get back inside?" I asked.

"Not until morning. I spent almost all night trying to unlock the door and not being

successful. By the time morning rolled around, the lock loosened just enough for me to unlock it and free the butler. He was extremely grateful," Mr. Chimes said.

"That's good," I said, "You won't believe this,"

"I think a female spirit lives in the room I stayed in. She's rather feisty," I said.

"Feisty how?"

"Well, she has a stomping problem and knocked a butler unconscious with a broom,"

"Wait what?" Mr. Chimes said, his eyes wide in disbelief.

"Yes. A female ghost knocked a butler unconscious,"

"Nothing of the sort has ever happened to me in *that* room. You must be special," Mr. Chimes said, with a wink.

"Special is a unique word," I said, "I think it's more like extremely unlucky,"

"Possibly. It depends on how you look at it. I'm going to get some coffee. Do you want some?" Mr. Chimes asked.

"Yes. I'd like coffee with a couple pumps of chocolate syrup, please," I said.

"Gotcha,"

When Mr. Chimes got back with two cups of steaming hot coffee, I continued my story.

"Before I came here for a night, I didn't even believe in ghosts, but now I'm questioning my own beliefs on whether ghosts are real or not. For instance, I felt as though I had a connection to the ghost in my room,"

"Katherine," Mr. Chimes said.

"You've met her?" I asked.

"Yes. She's strange,"

"What happened when you met her?"

"The faucet wouldn't turn off all night," Mr. Chimes said, "and like you said, she has a huge stomping problem and a door slamming problem,"

"I wonder what compels her to slam doors and stomp everywhere. Stomping can indicate anger," I said.

"You said you had to call two butlers last night for room service. Why did you have to call the second one?"

"The pipe broke, and a glass bottle broke in the closet," I said, "Also, the faucet got left on, somehow,"

I closed my eyes and shook my head as if clearing the memory from my head.

"Last night was all a blur. I can't believe half the things that happened last night," I said,   "But yet I know they're all real to an extent,"

I looked up to see Mr. Chimes's nose twitching again as he took another bite of food.

"That's weird. There's something about that room and faucets," Mr. Chimes said.

"My family and I used to come here every Halloween as I was growing up and I have to say we came home with LOTS of stories to tell. Legend has it that all the ghosts are more active around Halloween time,"

"Ohhh. I see," I said.

Ding. Ding. Ding. Rang Mr. Chimes pocket watch from inside his pocket.

"I'd better get going," Mr. Chimes said, "It was nice chatting with you. I hope you can get your night paid for soon,"

"Thanks. It was nice meeting you. Goodbye," I said, waving as I finished up the rest of my breakfast.

I headed towards the front door which was now unlocked. I tugged on it, but it still didn't budge. I tugged on it again, nothing. I stepped back to let other guests out of the hotel, they freely opened the door and headed out into the Salem streets, when I tried to follow them, an invisible barrier stopped me.

Mr. Chimes walked down the hallway, around a corner and out of sight.

ASPENS POV

Falling Through Time

We were falling down into the depths of numbers swirling all around us. It felt as if I was in a tornado that carried only numbers and wind, and the sounds clocks made as it swirled round and round. I started to get dizzy as we spiraled down into what seemed like a hole in a tree and rolled down a tunnel until finally, we rolled into a door that seemed to be built into a hollow of a tree. This door was miniature sized, possibly big enough for a rabbit. My huge hand knocked on the door and a small jar of juice appeared. It glowed orange and smelled of citrus.

"I think we have to drink this if we want to fit into this hollow," I said.

"What is it?" Fernando asked.

"I have no clue, smells like orange juice," I took a swig, and immediately coughed,   "Doesn't taste like orange juice though. That's disgusting,"

"Aspen, look at your finger," Fernando said, in shock. My finger had shrunk significantly. My arms began to shrink too, and I felt my whole body get smaller.

"I think you have to drink the potion to be my size. Otherwise, we'll never fit into this hollow," I called up to them as I got even smaller.

"Okay," Fernando said, seeming unsure. He took a swig followed by William, and they both shrunk to meet me at eye level. At the top of the hollow door was a plaque that read: *Timely Tree Hollow.*

I knocked again. A rustle sounded from behind the door, and it opened to reveal a white bunny with a twitching nose, wearing a pair of glasses, and a bunny sized suit with a golden chain hanging out of his right breast pocket.

"Hi, welcome to my humble home," The bunny said.

"Thank you," I said.

"Allow me to bring you up the stairs. The stew has just finished cooking. I can smell it from here," The bunny said, hopping up every step.

As we climbed a winding staircase, I noticed the wooden hollows of the tree had clocks of all different shapes and hung on it. It was as if the tree was a wall to decorate and hang items of significance on. Apparently, this bunny had a fondness for clocks. We kept climbing until we reached a hallway, and at the end of the hallway was a miniature kitchen, where another rabbit stood at the stove stirring a pot of delicious-smelling stew.

"Before we dine, allow me to show you where you'll be staying for your visit," The bunny said. He half walked, half hopped down a hallway adjacent to the kitchen and opened a door to reveal a small, yet cozy looking treehouse bedroom.

"Thank you, Mr……."

"Chimes," The bunny filled in.

"Would it be okay if I get some rest before supper?" William asked.

"Of course," Mr. Chimes said, "Everything you need is here. Anything you need and can't find, be sure to ask and my wife and I would be hoppy to help,"

I chuckled.

"William, your stardust should be arriving within a few minutes," I said.

"Sounds great. I've been looking forward to this all day," He said, yawning.

As we exited the room, I switched off the overhead lights so William could sleep. Just seconds later, a crow flew into the treehouse and dropped a miniature bottle of stardust in my hand. The blue glittery pieces of stardust seemed to shake in the bottle until I popped the lid off and walked back to the guest bedroom. William was already curled up in the twin bed, with the covers up to his shoulders. I tiptoed as quietly as I could to his bed and sprinkled some stardust on him. It seemed as if all the tensed up muscles in his face immediately relaxed and his shoulders relaxed downward. I looked down at the label which read: *Use this for a dreamless night of sleep. A little goes a long way. Love, Grandma Sandy.*

I turned on some music for William to listen to and slowly tiptoed out of the room again, trying hard not to wake him. He seemed to be deep in dreamland, and I was happy he was. He had needed rest within this wonderful rabbit's home which strangely felt like home to me too. I closed the door behind me as I slowly walked down the hallway to the kitchen to enjoy a warm, welcoming stew.

When I walked into the kitchen, I greeted Mr. and Mrs. Chimes and sat down at the table next to Fernando.

"So, what did I miss?" I asked Fernando.

"Nothing much. Is William sleeping?" Fernando asked.

"Yes. Tonight was the fastest he's fallen asleep in a while," I said.

Mr. and Mrs. Chimes seemed to be having a hushed conversation with their backs turned to us. They were hovering over the stove. Mrs. Chimes stirred the pot of stew while Mr. Chimes watched the timer as the last few seconds ticked by on the cornbread. I couldn't make out anything Mr. and Mrs. Chimes were saying but from their rapid hand gestures, and slightly raised voices, I could tell their conversation was getting intense.

Beep. Beep. Beep.

"The cornbread is done. We should eat," Mr. Chimes said.

"Okay. We're finishing our conversation later," Mrs. Chimes said, sternly.

Mr. Chimes brought the pan of homemade cornbread to the table, while Mrs. Chimes made bowls of stew. The bowls were white porcelain.

"Would one of you be so kind as to grab some silverware for

us?" Mrs. Chimes asked.

"Yes," I said, standing up.

"It's in the drawer by the sink. We need spoons, forks and a knife for the cornbread," Mrs. Chimes said.

"Got it," I said, grabbing the silverware and placing it on the table.

Mrs. Chimes placed the bowls on the table, and we all sat down to enjoy the meal. After we had said grace, I started by blowing on the steaming stew.

"So, what brings you to the Burrow tonight?" Mr. Chimes asked.

I looked at Fernando and he looked at me.

"Well, it's a little bit of a long story," Fernando said.

"Enlighten us," Mrs. Chimes said, taking a bite of stew.

"It all started when William started sleepwalking, and we heard him in the house. So, we followed him to Aspen's Grandma's house. Before we had even arrived there, her grandma had started some sort of potion to watch the dreams William was having. We made a stew called "Time to Think about Thyme Miso Soup," Fernando said.

"Allow me to add that this Miso Soup isn't just any soup. It was magical because with every bite we took, we created more of a golden key above the potion which glowed green and purple. The key we received was the key to open a pocket watch that wouldn't seem to stop ticking and then it opened, and we fell down the hole to this treehouse you call home," I added.

"The Burrow……. Is that what you call your home?" Fernando asked.

"The Burrow is a name for it," Mr. Chimes said.

"It's not fully our home. We travel often, so we have different homes in many different places. We say home is wherever the heart is," Mrs. Chimes said.

"Where do you like to go?" I asked.

"Just about anywhere," Mr. Chimes said, his nose twitching.

I have a feeling it's more than anywhere. He's hiding something.

"Cool," Fernando said.

"Do you like the stew?" Mrs. Chimes asked.

"Yes. Very much," I said.

"It's from a recipe that's been passed down through my family. I used to love it as a kid. In fact, my grandma would make this every time we came to visit," Mrs. Chimes said.

"That's a beautiful tradition," I said, smiling.

"I love this cornbread as well," Fernando said.

"Thanks!" Mr. Chimes said, "I've been messing with the recipe for a while trying to get the ratios of dry ingredients to wet ingredients just right. I think I've finally mastered the art of making cornbread, and besides, I could eat this stuff for days,"

"The last time my mom made cornbread, the whole pan was gone on the same day. It was so buttery, soft and comfortingly sweet that I couldn't stop eating it," I said.

"I have to say that your mom makes the best cornbread I've ever eaten," Fernando said, "It is not dry and crumbly, rather moist and sweet and stays together when you tear it apart,"

"I'll pass that on to her," I said.

"How is she, by the way?" Fernando asked.

"I don't know. We haven't been in touch recently. She should be arriving home with my dad from their cruise in about a day," I said.

"It's strange you haven't heard from them yet," Fernando said.

"Have you heard from your dad?" I asked.

"No. That's also strange. I would think that after he got back from the Salem Inn, he would at least text me or try to check in with me," Fernando said.

"That's rather interesting. You don't think it's possible that he never made it home, do you?" Mr. Chimes said.

I hadn't thought about that possibility and the many things it could mean until Mr. Chimes brought it up. *How did he seem to know something about William and Fernando's Dad, if he was completely uninvolved?*

"No. But why would he be stuck there?" I asked, confused.

"Maybe there's business that needs to be handled," Mr. Chimes said.

"He had the money to pay for the night we stayed there," Fernando said.

"Other business, I mean. Other than money," Mr. Chimes said.

"What business would that be?" I asked, taking another bite of stew.

"Alright…. That's a bit much for one night. We'd better be getting both of you to bed soon," Mrs. Chimes interjected.

Fernando took a bite of the cornbread on the table and sighed.

"This may be better than Aspen's moms," he said.

"Thank you," Mr. Chimes said.

"You two must be exhausted from your time traveling today," Mrs. Chimes said.

As if on cue, Fernando yawned.

"I'm tired. Nothing sounds better than a cozy bed and sleep,"

After seeing Fernando yawn, I yawned. My eyelids began to feel heavy.

"The powder room is the first door on your right and the guest room is at the end of the hallway," Mr. Chimes said, "Please make yourselves at home,"

I finished the last few bites of my stew.

"Do you want me to wash my bowl?" I asked.

"No, just leave it on the table, and we'll take care of it," Mr. Chimes said.

"Thank you for the wonderful meal," I said, "It was delicious,"

"Yes. Thank you. We'll see you in the morning," Fernando said, finishing his last few bites of cornbread.

"You're welcome," Mrs. Chimes said.

Fernando and I pushed our chairs in and headed to the bathroom which came with all the essentials. Everything we needed was inside. All the toiletries were even labeled with our names as if the Chimes had been expecting us. The bathroom only had one sink, one toilet, and one shower.

"Do you want the bathroom first?" Fernando asked.

"No, you go ahead. I'll go check in on William and get settled in the room. Take your time," I said.

"Thanks!" Fernando said. I closed the door behind me as I headed to the guest room and squinted into the darkness. I quietly opened one of the dressers to find clothes my size inside. *This is crazy.*

I lay in the twin bed and stared up at the ceiling for a little while, thinking about the confusing conversation we'd just had at dinner. *I wonder what business Mr. Lowell needs to attend to at the Salem Inn. Mr. and Mrs. Chimes know something about what he was doing there and the payment as well. I hope Mr. Lowell made it home safely, but at the same time if the house is haunted, maybe the Salem Inn is the safest place to be.* As my mind kept on spinning and wondering what Mr. and Mrs. Chime's motives were, my eyelids became heavier. I eventually gave into the rest that my body craved.

A short time later, somebody was poking my arm.

"Aspen. Wake up. It's your turn in the bathroom," Fernando whispered to me.

"Okay," I whispered back, slightly disoriented.

I padded my way to the bathroom and turned on the tap water to wash my face and brush my teeth. Then, I opened a drawer behind me, with my name on it in big cursive letters. Inside was a pair of cotton pajamas. The shirt was tie dyed light blue, the pants were light blue, and soft on the inside. I found a plush, blue, handknitted nightcap in the bottom of the drawer, pulled it over my head and walked back through the hallway. After I pulled the covers up to my chin, I turned towards the wall and slept soundly for many hours.

There was shuffling outside my door, and hushed voices conversed. I sat up in bed and listened. I still couldn't make out any words. It wasn't quite morning yet, so I laid back down. What seemed like a few minutes later, I heard the unmistakable constant ticking of Mr. Chimes's pocket watch, right outside our bedroom door. From across the room, I could see that Fernando had woken up too. He sat up in bed and tilted his head toward the door as if asking; d*o you want to go investigate?*

I nodded. We climbed out of bed and tip-toed toward the door. I opened the door to reveal no bunnies, but rather something different. Something interesting I'd never seen before. All the way down the hallway, there were what seemed like an endless supply of tiny doors, glowing on the outer perimeter. Each door had a year written on it in gold numbers. The dim amber glow of the hallway was almost mesmerizing.

One of the amber glowing doors clicked shut and seemed to naturally lock as it fell shut. I tried to open it, which confirmed my suspicions. I looked at the year on the door: 1823. *Why would the Chimes travel to 1823?*

"Pinch me," I whispered to Fernando, "Ouch,"

"This isn't a dream at all," Fernando whispered, "Look up,"

Above us was a display of stars of different colors: red, orange, yellow, and blue stars, some were large, and some were small. They all shone at different levels of brightness, the blue stars shining the brightest and the red stars the dimmest. I stood there in complete awe of the sky.

"Look, there's a rare purple star," Fernando said.

"You're right, how cool," I said.

We walked further down the hallway to find the wooden doors that had been there before we had fallen asleep still there. The tiny doors were somehow added in the darkness of the night. The tiny doors were shimmering like little speckles of light in the darkness of the hallway.

"Look, there's the moon," I said, pointing upwards towards the sky. The face of the man in the moon seemed to smile back down at us from above. The moonlight seemed to be part of the glow of the hallway as we continued to walk. The doors as we walked ascended in years on the right side and descended in years on the left side.

"Stop for a second," Fernando whispered, "Listen,"

I heard a gentle steady rhythm of something moving down the hall. *Hop! Hop! Hop!*

Tick. Tick. Tick.

"I think we've been found. What should we do?" I asked.

"Try to blend in," Fernando whispered.

We tried to hide in the nooks and crannies of the trees around us, while the moonlight and starlight gave us a shadow. I hoped none of this gave away our hiding spots. I felt someone tap me on the shoulder, turned around and jumped when I saw Fernando behind me. My heart pounded.

"What do you think you're doing?" I whisper-shouted.

"I think we have a problem," Fernando whisper shouted back.

Tick. Tick. Tick.

"Look," He whispered, pointing at a shadow from far away.

"That looks like a bunny," I whispered back to him.

"You don't think...,"

"I do," I said, nodding.

"Come on," Fernando whispered, grabbing my hand and running toward a glowing door that appeared to be attached to a tree house.

The ticks grew faster. More rapid.

"Locked," He whispered.

I pulled on the doorknob, jiggled it and it slowly creaked open.

"What are you two doing out of bed in the middle of the night?" Mr. Chimes asked, crankily.

"We.........um.........heard movement in the hall and were curious," I said.

"I see. You'd better get back to bed soon, otherwise, you may have to come with me on some of my travels," Mr. Chimes said.

"Okay," Fernando said, scurrying down the hallway and into our bedroom again. I followed suit, laid down in bed, closed my eyes and drifted off thinking, *what would be so bad about time traveling?*

The next morning, the smell of bacon pulled me from my deep slumber. William and Fernando had already woken up and had some quiet time in bed while they waited for me to wake up. William was reading a book, and Fernando was watching a show on his phone in silence. I stretched and sat up in bed.

"Look who finally decided to finally wake up, Sleeping Beauty," William teased.

"Shut up," I said, grumpily. In return, he chucked a pillow at me, which missed by a few feet. I laughed. Fernando grinned.

"I'm happy you're awake, Prince Charming," Fernando said to William.

"I'm glad I slept so well. I needed every second of that long night's slumber," William said.

"Okay. Let's go eat some bacon. I'm starving," I said.

"Me too," William said.

"I'll bet. Dinner last night was stew and cornbread, so you didn't miss out on much," I said.

"Cornbread!?" William said.

"Yes,"

"I love cornbread. Are there leftovers?"

"Yes. There are maybe one or two pieces left," I said.

We headed to the table which had been extended to accommodate all five of us. The table was now rectangular instead of square.

"Good morning," Mr. Chimes said warmly as the three of us sat down. He acted as though nothing had happened last night, and he wasn't the slightest bit mad at us.

"Good morning," We replied.

Mrs. Chimes stood over a pancake griddle flipping a batch of banana chocolate chip pancakes. Mr. Chimes had bacon sizzling in a pan on the left burner on the stove and eggs cooking in a separate pan on the burner next to the bacon.

"That bacon is what got me out of bed this morning," I said.

"It smells amazing," William said.

"Thank you!" Mr. Chimes said, flipped the bacon.

"How many pancakes do you all want?" Mrs. Chimes asked.

"Three," I said.

"Four," William said.

"Three," Fernando said.

"Bring your plates right over and I'll serve you," Mrs. Chimes said.

At the center of the table sat a stack of plates. They were all white with a floral design on the outside. Mr. Chimes flipped the over easy eggs he was cooking and served up the bacon. He asked all of us how many we wanted and served it up. He brought the eggs to the table and gave each of us two eggs, then headed back to the counter to build his own plate, followed by Mrs. Chimes.

We all sat down, said grace and then dug into our breakfast.

"Where did you all learn how to cook?" I asked.

"Many places. I think you learn a little something from every cook you meet," Mrs. Chimes said.

"That makes sense," I said, "Every cook has a different

technique, and style of cooking that you had never thought of before,"

"Exactly," Mrs. Chimes said.

I took another bite of pancake and chewed thoughtfully. The pancake was sweet, buttery, and fully satisfied my cravings bite and the subtle savory flavor of the eggs had balanced out my sweet cravings. The meal was a little sweet, savory, salty, smoky.

"So, we have lots of possibilities of where this day could take us," Mr. Chimes said.

"We could do a tour of the house," Mrs. Chimes suggested.

"Let's do it," Mr. Chimes said.

"I wonder what we might find," William said.

"We'll just have to wait and see," I said.

"Then, we can do a cooking lesson for supper," Mrs. Chimes said.

"Really!?" I asked, lighting up in excitement.

"Of course. It's about time for you to learn how to make our delicious stew. You boys can help with the bread," Mrs. Chimes said.

"Let's go!" Fernando said enthusiastically, doing a secret handshake with William.

"Do you all have syrup?" William asked.

"Yes, in the fridge in the door on your right," Mr. Chimes said.

"Found it," William said, walking back to the table and sitting down. He drizzled some syrup on his pancakes and took another bite. I could tell by his sigh of contentment that he absolutely loved them.

"Did you sleep okay, William?" Mr. Chimes asked.

"Yes. That bed is so comfortable," William said.

"Good. I'm glad you slept through the night; unlike some other people I saw walking down the hall last night," Mr. Chimes said, furrowing his eyebrows, frowning.

"We're sorry. We were just curious," Fernando said. I held my breath, waiting for him to scold us for being out of bed when we weren't supposed to be.

"I'm just messing with you," Mr. Chimes said, chuckling.

"You were up last night?" William asked.

"Yeah, just for a little bit. We heard the pocket watch and a little shuffling in the hallway and wanted to go investigate," I explained

"What did you see?" William asked.

"So many things. The stars, and tiny doors with years engraved on them in gold. The outside edges of the doors glowed. It seemed as though the hallway of doors never ended," Fernando said.

"Interesting," William said.

After we had all finished eating, we got ready and cleaned up the kitchen we met in the small living area we had tumbled into on our first night.

"Now," Mr. Chimes began, "Before I start this tour, I want to ask you a few questions,"

"First, before you fell through the pocket watch portal, did you think this tree was small?"

"Yes. Then, we drank the orange stuff and shrank down small enough to fit into the hollow again," I said.

"What was that orange stuff by the way?" Fernando asked.

"Shrinking SunnyD," Mr. Chimes replied.

"No wonder it looked like orange juice," Fernando said, amused.

"The stairs are the key to what is about to blow your mind. This hollow is bigger than you might think," Mr. Chimes said, "How did your tumble down to the common area of the hollow start?"

"Down a tunnel," I said.

"Right on,"

"Let's start with this common area," Mr. Chimes said, gesturing around the living space which you entered into before the kitchen. On his left was a cozy looking couch, by a fireplace with a few blankets hung on the back of the couch. On either side of the couch, at an angle, were two chairs that faced the mantel.

"As you can probably tell, we enjoy having fires in the wintertime," Mr. Chimes said.

"How does your treehouse not burn down?" I asked.

"We have a small chimney. You likely didn't see it on the way in because you were falling down the rabbit hole,"

"Now, we have the kitchen, which you are all very familiar with," Mr. Chimes said.

There was a stove on the wall next to the refrigerator. Beside the stove were drawers and cabinets. Directly across from the refrigerator was the dishwasher, and next to the dishwasher were more cabinets. I liked the layout of the kitchen. It fit the space very well. In the center of all the appliances, cabinets and shelves were the tables we had dined at.

"Next, we'll be showing you what's behind the doors of the rest of the rooms in this hallway. But first, here's the layout," Mr. Chimes said.

As he talked, I noticed that the ceiling had returned, and the glowing doors had entirely disappeared in the daylight. It had to be *nighttime* to travel in time. That's why we arrived at the Hollow at *night.*

"I zoned out, sorry," I whispered to Fernando, "What was he telling us again?"

"There are five rooms we need to see in this hallway. The sixth room is a boring one: the Chimes's room. It's the wooden door all the way at the end," Fernando whispered to me as I trailed behind the group.

"Here's the first room. Any guesses what's behind this door?" Mr. Chimes said.

"A garden?" I asked.

"Yes," Mr. Chimes said.

Ohhhhh. That's why there's a window in the closet to help the plants grow.

We walked into the hot, humid greenhouse and looked at the plants the Chimes grew. The whole room seemed to be an endless array of beautiful plants. The plants seemed to stretch as far as the eye could see. The dome above us was of the beautiful night sky. All the plants grew beautifully in moonlight and starlight. The plants almost seemed to glow under the dim lighting, and I soaked up the beauty around me.

"Feel free to look around," Mrs. Chimes said.

"This makes me think of the ocean, if it was made of plants," I said.

"Yes. But there aren't any waves," Fernando said.

"Use your imagination,"

"Maybe the different heights of the plants could look like waves,"

"True. Interesting thought," I said, as I continued to look around.

I walked slowly up and down the aisles of potted plants she grew and saw names of plants I'd never heard of before. I saw a tag that read: Ipomoea batatas, Capsicum annuum, Cucumis sativus, Cucurbita pepo, Cucurbita pepo, Agaricus bisporus; Daucus carota, and so many more.

"Daucus carota has to be our favorite of the plants in our greenhouse," Mrs. Chimes said.

"That's so cool," I said.

Above the plant rows, there were shelves with mini jars of many different colors of dust. There were red dusty substances with tags on them with names I could not pronounce. Next to the red substances were orange puffy dust substances with names written in what seemed like a different language. Underneath a star was a yellow shiny dust, and underneath another star was a blue dust that seemed to glow and glitter whenever light bounced off of it.

On the next wall over was a shelf of more plants with labels reading: Anethum graveolens, Osmium Basilica, Origanum vulgare, Allium sphenogram, Thymus vulgaris, Salvia Rosmarinus, Matricaria chamomilla, Mentha, Melissa officinalis, Jasminum, and so many more. I stared in wonder and awe at all these thriving plants and this beautiful greenhouse that I didn't even know existed on the other side of the treehouse until now.

I bent my head down to smell the flower of a bolting Matricaria chamomilla plant. I closed my eyes, and the scent made me think of my dad. I remembered my bedroom as a child and the cushioned rocking chair he would always sit in to read me a book before bed. Every time he walked into the room, he had a mug of chamomile tea. Sometimes he squeezed lemon juice and honey into the tea. I remember the scent of chamomile tea meaning it was time to drift away into a dream world. I remember watching the steam rise off the tea and listening to my dad's soothing voice as my eyelids would grow heavy and I would drift away to sleep. I sighed as the memory rested on my spirit and exhaled as I moved onto the wildflower collection in the greenhouse.

I recognized the daisies, tulips, and baby miniature sunflowers almost immediately. Every single detail of the same type of every flower was always unique and intriguing. Some sunflowers grew in many different varieties. Some of them had a yellow middle, and yellow pedals. Some had brown middles, and dark red pedals. Some had almost "furry" looking pedals with a yellow middle. Sunflowers, like people, are all unique in their own way, yet we like sunflowers always strive for the light. We always try to reach the light, but we can only grow so tall.

Someone tapped me on my shoulder.

"Are you ready?" Fernando asked.

"Yes," I said, still slightly lost in my thoughts.

"We're off to the clock room next," Mr. Chimes said, walking further down the hallway and turning the doorknob.

The tick tock sound hit me almost immediately. I was overwhelmed, almost dizzy by how much the clocks were ticking. My head pounded with all the dings, dongs, ticks and hands swirling around the clocks. It became blurry very quickly and I blinked trying to recover my vision. I covered my ears and William and Fernando followed suit. Mr. Chimes pressed a button on his pocket watch and the clocks froze mid sound, which felt blissful.

"This is my clock room, where I keep all my most prized clocks," Mr. Chimes said, "Feel free to look at all of them, and join me back by the door,"

On all the walls except the wall with the door hung all types of clocks. Cuckoo clocks, bird analog clocks, golden analog clocks, silver analog clocks, tick tock clocks, digital clocks, and so many more. The clock that appeared the most was probably the cat co-co clocks with tails and eyes moving back and forth with every tick and every tock. It felt creepy because it felt like all the clocks were watching me. Goosebumps trickled up my back and down my arms.

"Let's get out of here," I said.

"Great idea," William said.

"I second that," Fernando said, "This is creepy,"

"The next room is the tearoom," Mr. Chimes said, opening the door to the room with a three on the door.

The tearoom had shelves on all four walls, and all types of tea such as Chamomile, Jazzmine, Black tea, Earl Gray, Green, Fireside Spice, Cardamom, Chai, Strawberry Green tea, and so many more.

There was a circular table in the center. On top of the table was a porcelain teapot with flower decals all over the outside. The four teacups that were placed in a circle around it had flower decals along the rim. Four white plates were placed at each spot with a comfy, plush chair behind it.

On the tables were an assortment of finger sandwiches and freshly picked berries. Next to the berries there were freshly baked cinnamon rolls and freshly brewed tea.

"Can we have a cinnamon roll?" I asked, eyeing the delicious looking roll.

"Yes, why don't you try a tea as well?" Mr. Chimes said.

"Which tea would you recommend?"

"I like so many different types of tea. One of my personal favorites is strawberry hibiscus,"

"I'll try that one then," I said, grabbing a cinnamon roll off the platter.

"Coming right up," Mr. Chimes said, putting water on the stove to boil.

"These cinnamon rolls are really good,"

"Mrs. Chimes made them. Tell her,"

"Will do. The frosting is so warm and gooey,"

"She's a great cook," Mr. Chimes said.

"Indeed. Thanks for the tea," I said, as Mr. Chimes handed me a steaming mug of tea.

"Think about the meaning of tea," Mr. Chimes said, as we exited the room.

What about tea does he want us to figure out?

The next room we visited was the room at the end of the hallway: the Chimes's bedroom. It was a large bedroom with a bed in the center. On either side of the bed frame was a nightstand with a small pocket watch sitting on it. Each of the pocket watches was open yet not making any noise. Above the bed on the wall hung a huge black and white clock. The walls were painted a sky-blue color, which seemed to relax me. Inside their room was a walk-in closet and a bathroom. On their wall across from their bed, hung a compass frame. *Interesting. It's as if time is your compass. Time guides you to where you need to go.*

Underneath the compass rose was a message: *May your heart always guide you.*

"This is our bedroom. Feel free to have a look, and then we're moving onto my favorite part of the tour," Mr. Chimes said.

We headed onto the next room where a TV powered off sat in the center of the room with a couch across from it.

"Try to use your phone in here," Mr. Chimes said.

I tried to use my phone, and it wouldn't turn on. Neither would William's or Fernando's.

"They won't turn on," I said.

"Let me show you why," Mr. Chimes said, clicking the power button on the remote.

At first the TV screen glowed a blinding white, and I squeezed my eyes shut. Then I tried to squint at the TV. Mrs. Chimes, who had followed us to the back of the room, clicked the lights off and the blinding white light dimmed slightly as our eyes adjusted.

"Aspen, what's your house number?" Mr. Chimes asked.

"1429," I said.

Mr. Chimes clicked a few buttons on the remote and then hit enter and the TV screen showed my house. It was empty on the inside, a broken glass on the floor, no sound coming from the house. It seemed like nobody was home, which worried me.

"Woah. You're telling me that my house number gives you access to look at what is happening in my house at any time," I said, shocked.

"Yes. It also gives you access to look at what's happening in the lives of loved ones. The numbers on the remote are also letters if you press the shift button," Mr. Chimes said.

"That's so cool," Fernando said, "How can we pull up our dad?"

"All I need is your dad's first name," Mr. Chimes said.

"John," William said.

"5646," Mr. Chimes said, typing in the numbers.

The TV blinked for a minute before focusing on a solemn looking Mr. Lowell who was stuck in a bedroom that looked strangely like the room, we had stayed in at the Salem inn.

"He's not trapped in there is he?" I said, concern etched all over my face.

"I hope not. I think that's the Salem Inn," WIlliam said, "Look, there's the Innkeeper at the door,"

"He's so creepy," Fernando said, shuddering.

"Wait. Look!" I said, pointing at the screen.

"Did you just see that?" I asked.

The balcony door had opened and slammed shut again all on its own. Then, the screen went black.

"No, I missed it," William said.

"I saw it. What if there's a ghost haunting Mr. Lowell?" Fernando asked.

"I don't know. Maybe," William said.

"Why did the TV turn off?" I asked.

"Because of the different energies in the atmosphere," Mr. Chimes said.

"Which energies?" I asked.

"Whenever there are bad energies interfering with our connection between different data signals, it cancels out the good energies, which results in no connection," Mr. Chimes said.

"What defines energies as bad or good?" I asked.

"That's rather complicated," Mr. Chimes said, "because there's bad, good and everything in between. Sometimes the connection is glitchy because the energies are in that gray space in between bad and good, rather neutral or part of both,"

I furrowed my eyebrows as I pondered this. I never thought data connection could be part of bad and good energy. Growing up, I'd always thought that data connection, data, and power ran from electricity on from power lines. Whenever the power lines fell down due to a bad storm it resulted in no power because of the broken electrical current flowing through the line. But this power source was something different entirely.

The TV could watch other people but only if the energies were just right in the location you wanted to watch them in. The energies didn't come from powerlines, rather people, spirits, and the molecular forces around us that shape us as human beings. The house was beginning to expand my horizons and change the way I used to think about many things.

"Time to move on to the last room," Mr. Chimes said.

"Okay," I said, numbly as I was still lost in thought.

"This last room is not a room, rather a network of rooms," Mr. Chimes said, "Remember what I was saying in the beginning about this place being bigger than you originally thought,"

Mr. Chimes opened the door, switched on the light and gestured for us to follow him down a wooden spiral staircase. The light wasn't a lightbulb, instead it was a glowing torch illuminating the staircase every few feet. By the time we made it down all the way to the bottom, I looked up to see four trees all growing towards a dark, starry sky.

"This is what I like to call my tree garden," Mr. Chimes said gesturing around the room.

"Woah," I said, looking up towards the glowing moon.

"Let me show you a few things," Mr. Chimes said.

We followed Mr. Chimes towards an orange tree in the center of the room, surrounded by a short golden wall of sorts. Underneath our feet the floor after the wooden staircase was made of the softest moss I'd ever felt. It tickled my toes as I walked and squished every now and then. I didn't mind the dampness under my feet. All I cared about in this moment was how wonderful all this was. I was captivated by the wonder of a whole different world that surrounded me.

"This, my friends, is the center tree," Mr. Chimes said, pointing at the orange tree which stood in front of me. It was many feet taller than the rest of the trees in the tree garden. The orange tree seemed to glow fluorescently in the moonlight. The brightest part of the tree was the oranges that seemed to glow in the moonlight from above.

"This tree grows on very fertile soil and thrives with great fruit. We love savoring the fruit this tree provides us with," Mr. Chimes said.

At the center of the garden was the orange tree, with three trees surrounding it. Each tree around the orange tree was different. I identified the one to the right of the orange tree as an oak tree from the pointy, smooth, green leaves. The one to the left of the orange tree was a maple based on the five points of the leaves. The last tree behind the orange tree was a pine tree which stood out to me because all the other trees had actual leaves, but the pine tree just had needles.

"Feel free to walk around and explore. Please don't touch the trees. They're rather precious to me," Mr. Chimes said.

As I walked around, I read the label marker plate nailed into the golden wall surrounding all the trees. The label on the wall surrounding the pine tree said, "Piersons" on the label. *Hmm. What was wrong with my plant identification?* I looked up into the pine tree and saw little lanterns with candles in them. Each branch had a different number of lanterns on it. At the very tippy top, there were only two and it eventually trickled down branch by branch. Each flame bobbed up and down as air circulated through the tree garden.

I walked towards the Maple tree next and saw the same candlelit lanterns in this tree. The maple tree had many more lanterns than the pine tree and a different array of branches coming from the tree. The right side of this tree was larger than the left, due to the larger number of branches more candlelit flames sat on top of the branches. *How do these trees not burn down? I wonder if they're enchanted somehow.* The marker of the Maple tree read: Ropes.

"Wait a minute," I said, everything starting to click in my head.

"Mr. Chimes," I called.

"Yes?" He said, walking towards me.

"This tree isn't what I think it is, is it?" I asked, shocked.

"Trust your instinct," he said, with a wink.

"It is my family tree, then. I can't believe it," I said shrieking in excitement, overjoyed.

"This must be ours then," William said, pointing to the oak tree. The marker on the low golden wall read: Lowell.

"You're right. This room of my house is my favorite part of the whole house because it lets me tap into emotions that are not my own. For example, did you know that each flame on the branches of the trees represents a different person? And each flame on the tree glows a different color based on how that person is feeling?" Mr. Chimes asked, pointing to the Ropes's family tree.

All the flames that represented people from the same family tree glowed a neon color that was mixed with a pastel color. Some were red, some were dark orange, some were blue.

"Wow," I said, awestruck by the colors I saw and the magic

around me.

"What do all the colors mean?" William asked.

"You'll have to interpret as you see necessary. Different colors mean different things to different people,"

The oak tree was different from all the rest. Instead of the lanterns floating above the branches, they were hung underneath the branches with different brightly colored fabric which glowed in the moonlight. The flames on the oak tree were dimmer than all the rest and looked very close to going out.

"Why are the flames dimmer than the rest of the trees?" I asked.

"You'll just have to wait and see," Mr. Chimes said.

Circling back around to the front of the room, I found the same lanterns on the orange tree, but this one seemed to have the fewest lanterns, and the fewest branches. One lantern in particular burned brightly, so I looked away from the bright light to see another light this time on the Oak Lowell tree. *Hmm. Interesting. Are these families connected somehow?*

Ring. Ring. Ring.

"It's getting late, we'd better be heading back upstairs to make supper," Mr. Chimes said.

"That tour took all day?" Fernando asked, as we followed Mr. Chimes back up the spiral staircase. From behind us, I heard William kick something hard that was raised from the surface of the moss floor.

"Yes, they do say time flies when you're having fun," Mr. Chimes replied.

"Ouch," he said, looking down to see what he had stubbed his toe on.

"You okay?" I asked him as we followed Fernando and Mr. Chimes up the stairs.

"Yeah. Don't know what I stubbed my toe on though," William said.

"Maybe a rock?" I suggested.

"Maybe," William said, unsure.

"What day is it anyway?" Fernando asked.

"I honestly don't know," Mr. Chimes said, "I can show you

something when we get back upstairs to tell you the time and date,"

"Can't we just use our phones?" William asked.

"No. Bad cell reception because of different energies, remember?" Fernando said, trying to turn his phone on. It didn't light up when he pressed the power button.

How am I supposed to check in with my parents when they get home?

Mr. Chimes brought all of us back into the last room we'd been in. Inside was the TV and sofa directly across from it. He picked up the remote, pressed the power button and then pressed a few buttons on the remote. The TV immediately showed the day of the week and date in bold white letters and numbers. The date was 11/7/2024, and the day of the week was Thursday.

"Aspen, your parents should be home by now," William said, furrowing his brow in concern.

"Let's program it to my house," I said, determined to prove that my parents had made it home safely.

"Remind me of your house number," Mr. Chimes said.

"1429," I said.

Once again, the TV screen showed my house as empty. No sound came from the house, and there were no cars parked in the driveway. It was entirely vacant. Pluto wasn't even inside.

"What about Pluto?" I asked.

"Let's type him into the TV system,"

This time, the TV showed a moving bouncing vision of trees.

"He must have escaped the house," I said, and the screen went black once again.

"I'm going to prepare the kitchen for supper. Join me when you're ready," Mr. Chimes said.

As soon as Mr. Chimes left the room, I asked, "What should we do?" My parents should have arrived home a few days ago. I don't know why they didn't,"

There are a dozen possibilities. I hope their ship didn't malfunction and start sinking. That would be bad. What would I do without them?

"I think we just need to wait it out, after we figure out how to travel back through time to your house," Fernando said.

"Good point. We have no clue what the portal to home is," William said.

"For now, Aspen, I think we're going to have to trust that the universe will deliver us to wherever we need to be whenever we need to be there," Fernando said.

"Okay," I said, taking a deep breath.

"Somehow I feel like we were meant to fall through space and time and end up here," William said.

"I know exactly what you mean," I said.

"It feels like we've known Mr. and Mrs. Chimes for longer than a day, yet we've only just met them," Fernando said.

"Speaking of the Chimes, we'd better go meet them to cook dinner,"

When we made it to the kitchen, we greeted Mr. and Mrs. Chimes.

"Hi! Welcome to your cooking lesson. We'll start with the stew and cook the bread while we wait for the stew to simmer down. First, we'll need to do some harvesting," Mrs. Chimes said.

She handed William a basket and told him to harvest three Ipomoea batatas.

"I'll come with you," I said, following WIlliam down the hallway and into the garden room. Once again, it was so beautiful it took my breath away.

"I think I remember where they are," William said, walking towards a table row.

"Right here," I said, pointing to the potato-like root vegetable poking out of the soil.

"I guess we have to pull them up," William said, grabbing the roots and pulling on it.

One potato came up out of the ground. William placed it into the basket and grabbed two more out of the same bin.

"This plant never seems to end," William said, gesturing toward the potatoes already regrowing where the ones we had just harvested were.

"That's interesting," I said.

"Indeed," William said.

As we walked back towards the door gently cradling the potatoes, William tripped over something he hadn't seen on the ground before.

"Aspen. Come here," William said, crouching down to uncover what he had just tripped on. He moved the fake grass of the greenhouse room aside to reveal a handle.

"It's a trap door," I said, "That's surprising, yet makes sense because Mr. and Mrs. Chimes need rabbit holes to travel through. These probably go down into a network of tunnels they dug themselves,"

"You're right, but we have one problem though,"

"What's that?"

"It won't open," William said.

"That's too bad," I said, "We'd better head back to the kitchen before Mr. and Mrs. Chimes suspect something's up,"

We headed back to the kitchen to find Fernando carefully, precisely chopping an onion with slightly teary eyes. Mrs. Chimes stood next to him stirring and measuring the spices that needed to be put into the stew. I saw salt, pepper, cumin, and turmeric in the jars to her left. I assumed she had more to add to the three separate bowls of spices in front of her. One jar was a bright yellow sparkly powder that didn't stop sparkling until it was mixed in with the rest of the spices.

"Aspen, add some oil, onions, and garlic to the pan, would you please?" Mrs. Chimes asked, gesturing to the pan on the stove.

"I'm on it," I said.

"William, can you please peel and cut the sweet potatoes and carrots, then add them to the pan with the garlic and onion?" Mrs. Chimes asked.

The pan on the stove was hot, sizzling and steaming. It sizzled more when William added the thinly sliced carrots and sweet potatoes.

"Fernando, can you stir this for about five minutes?" Mrs. Chimes asked.

"You got it,"

"Thanks. I'll go grab the flour for the bread we're making

tonight," Mrs. Chimes said.

She hopped around the corner and out of sight. As Fernando stirred the stew, the fragrant scents wafted around the kitchen, and I started to feel tired. The long day of exploring the Chimes's house was fun, but I was also looking forward to a good night's rest.

Mr. Chimes sat in his chair by the hearth, and read what looked like a newspaper, and Mrs. Chimes arrived back with a large bag of flour. The timer went off indicating we could move on to the next step.

"I need somebody to dump the can of tomatoes into the pot. Then, I need all three of you to add your third of the spice mixture at the same time," Mrs. Chimes said.

We obliged. Fernando dumped the can of diced tomatoes into the pot, and we counted to three together. On three we dumped the bowl of spices each of us held into the pot. The pot began to bubble furiously before calming down to a gentle simmer.

"We need to wait twenty-five minutes for that to simmer down before we add the spinach, then we're done with the stew," Mrs. Chimes said, "In the meantime, we're going to start on the bread rolls,"

"We're making cheesy garlic herb bread tonight," Mrs. Chimes said, pulling a skillet out from the cabinet underneath the stove.

Cheesy Garlic Herb Bread

Ingredients
3 cups all-purpose flour
3 tablespoons sugar
1 tablespoon baking powder
2 teaspoons Italian seasoning
1 teaspoon garlic powder
1/2 teaspoon salt
1 large egg, room temperature
1 cup fat-free milk
1/3 cup canola oil
1 cup shredded sharp cheddar cheese

1) Preheat oven to 350°. In a large bowl, whisk together

first 6 ingredients. In another bowl, whisk together egg, milk and oil. Stir in cheese and add to flour mixture; stir just until moistened.

2) Spoon batter into a greased 9-in. cast-iron skillet and bake at 350° until a toothpick inserted in center comes out clean, 25-30 minutes.

"I need someone to mix dry ingredients and someone to mix wet ingredients,"

"I'll do the wet," I said.

"I'll do the dry," Fernando said.

"And I'll pop it into the oven," William said.

"Perfect," Mrs. Chimes said.

"Aspen, your ingredients are right here. You have flour, sugar, baking powder, Italian seasoning, garlic powder, and salt. The amount you're supposed to add is listed on this card," Mrs. Chimes said, "Be sure to measure carefully,"

"Fernando, your wet ingredients are an egg, oil, and fat free milk. Whisk them well and then dump the wet ingredients into the dry ingredients," Mrs. Chimes instructed.

Fernando nodded and started by cracking the egg sitting on the counter on the side of the bowl.

"William, please butter the pan and turn the burner on medium high heat,"

William obliged just in time for Fernando and I to finish mixing the dry and wet ingredients together to form a dough which we poured straight into the already warm pan.

"Now, we let that sit for twenty to thirty minutes," Mrs. Chimes said.

"Great job," I said to my sous-chefs.

"You too," Fernando said.

"Thanks," I said, as we all sat at the kitchen table waiting for everything to cook.

As time ticked by, I felt my eyelids growing heavier and heavier. I yawned a couple of times and grew very tired. I could see that William and Fernando felt the same way based on how they just stared into space seeming disinterested in the activity that was going on around them. Time seemed to slowly drift by like a piece of wood on a river's current.

Other than the slight sizzle of the stew and the bubbling of the bread, the house was the quietest it had been all day. I loved the stimulating quiet of the kitchen, because the sights and smells of the food that was being prepared always smelled heavenly and looked beyond delicious. The slight sizzle of the pots on the stovetop relaxed me and I felt myself craving sleep, yet fighting the urge to close my eyes.

Ring! Ring!

"The soup is done," Mrs. Chimes said.

"I'll dish it up," William said.

"I'll start with the bread that will be done in a few more minutes," Mr. Chimes said, when William tried to pass him a bowl.

"Same here," Mrs. Chimes said.

"Suit yourself. This stew looks pretty delicious to me," William said.

He handed me a bowl of the warm steaming stew, and I walked over to the table, with Fernando following behind me. William made himself a bowl and sat down. We all held hands, said grace and started on the stew.

Ring! Ring!

"That's the bread," Mr. Chimes said, taking it off the burner. He cut himself a rather large piece and sat down with us at the table, nibbling at the bread. Mrs. Chimes cut herself a normal sized piece and sat next to him.

I blew on the sweet potato stew and took a bite. It was so warm and comforting, it felt like a cozy blanket I would cover up with in the wintertime right before sleep. I took bite after bite, and it seemed as if after every bite I took more cozy warm thoughts floated into my head. A warm fireplace on a cold winter's day. A cozy, plush bed where I could rest my tired body and mind. A warm fire outside on a crisp fall evening. A warm cup of tea in my hands. A warm cup of hot cocoa while watching the snow fall outside my window.

After finishing the stew, I said, "Good night everyone. I'm

exhausted,"

I walked towards our guest room and heard a pair of footsteps following me. I turned around to find that William was following me, and Fernando was behind him. We all climbed into bed without hitting the powder room beforehand or even thinking about doing so. We just wanted, and received rest, comfort and calm. That is until we heard heavy footsteps walking across the room and repeating the same words over and over again.

"Follow me. Trap door,"

"William. What do you think you're doing? You know we shouldn't be up this late," I said, shaking his shoulders. His eyes seemed to be glossed over, and he looked at me, confused.

"He's sleepwalking," Fernando whispered, "I've never seen it this bad before,"

"Trap. Door," William said, turning the doorknob and walking down the hallway. Fernando and I ran after him. He was all the way down the staircase in the tree room before he tripped on a knob sticking up amidst the moss in front of the orange tree. I kept running as I saw him fall towards the moss floor, until there wasn't a moss floor beneath him any longer. It had vanished to reveal a black hole that William fell straight into. The black hole started to close once again after William had fallen far enough down.

"William must have twisted the knob to open the trap door with his foot or something. I need to go rescue him," Fernando said, panicked.

"I'm coming with you," I said.

As soon as I jumped into the black hole, it closed above me, and everything disappeared into darkness.

A man wearing glasses, dressed in a nice suit is walking down the street past the graveyard. The click clack of his shoes fall in tempo with the constant ticking of the pocket watch he has tucked into his right pocket. He stops one street before the Ropes Mansion, opens the pocket watch and turns down a separate street. He walks by a graveyard on his right. Walks a little way and then turns again as if his pocket watch was his navigation system, or he was paranoid about being late.

"Wrong turn," He mutters to himself, turns around and sees that I'm following him.

"William. What brings you here today?" He asked.

Silence. I try to speak but I can't. I mouth the one word that comes to mind: Lost.

"Let time guide you," He said, "You'll see,"

I nod. I mouth another word that comes to mind: Mother.

"Time will guide you," He replies, picking up on my word instantly.

```
SALEM MASSACHUSETTS
1860, October 30th
William POV
```

The steady hand of someone touching my wrist slowly began to bring me back to reality. I heard the shuffling of people around me and the air smelled of blood. I blinked my eyes open and didn't recognize my surroundings. I was in a large room that was rectangular with many beds lined up on both of the longer walls. The man lying in the bed next to me had a large bloody gash running from his shoulder down to his elbow, and his right leg had been bandaged to no avail. Blood was starting to seep out of the bandage.

"Sir," The nurse said to the man next to me, "We need to give you stitches. Bite down on this rag. Here's a bottle of medicine to help with the pain,"

He took the bottle and drank rapidly as the nurse worked quickly to sew up his wounds.

All around me, there were people sleeping. Others were coughing uncontrollably.

"Tuberculosis," A doctor whispered to a nurse near my bed, "Extremely contagious,"

The nurse who had taken my pulse smiled down at me, and said, "Pulse is normal,"

The doctor wrote that down. I tried to touch my head, which was pounding.

"We'll give you a cool rag to help with the pain," The nurse said.

"Thanks," I said, slurring my speech slightly. The burning, swollen sensation in my throat caused a coughing fit. I tried to start another sentence, but my voice was hoarse, so I closed my eyes and rested until a cool rag was placed on my forehead.

"How are you doing?" The nurse asked.

I gave her a thumb to the side. *Can't talk.* I mouthed.

"Drink this," The nurse said, "for the pain,"

"What's your name?" I whispered, hoarsely. I never heard her response before falling back into a deep slumber.

Sometime later, I heard a boy's voice somewhere in the distance.

"Where is he? I need to see him,"

I sat up in bed to find that my head wasn't pounding any longer and my body felt much better. I was bigger than I had been at the hollow, yet the same size as everyone around me. *How did I grow to be so big?*

"He's right here," the same nurse as before said.

"William," A boy and girl who looked vaguely familiar said at the same time, relieved.

"Who are you, again?"

The boy and girl looked at each other with worried expressions on their faces.

"I'm Fernando, your brother," The boy said.

"I'm Aspen, your good friend," The girl said.

"And where did I meet you?" I asked, still confused.

"Give us one minute," The girl said.

They talked with hushed voices with their backs turned to me, but loud enough for me to hear them.

"What do we do?" The girl asked the boy.

"I don't know. I can't believe William doesn't remember I'm his brother,"

"I think we need to get him somewhere away from the hospital and then we can make a plan as to how we're going to fix this,"

The girl spoke with the nurse and the boy came back over to my bedside.

"How are you feeling?" He asked.

I shrugged. I didn't feel as though I could trust this boy yet. He seemed overly caring and compassionate towards me, and I didn't know why. I tried to think of any lasting memory I had of this boy that I thought I recognized from somewhere, but I didn't know where. I tried to think back to the last memory I had of him and came up empty. What I remember is how tender and caring everyone was towards me throughout this journey of healing. I felt warmed by the sympathy I received.

"I hope you feel better soon," he said, cringing as we heard the man a few beds down vomit into a pail.

"Okay. You're discharged. We're using this wheelchair to take you somewhere," The girl said.

"I can walk," I said, trying to stand up. The world seemed to blur around me, and I felt someone's hands catch me before I fell back down to the floor.

"No, you most definitely cannot," the nurse said.

I only faintly heard her next sentence, "There's an inn just around the corner. Take him there and let him sleep off the medicine. When he wakes, give him another fifteen millitters of this,"

Then, my eyes closed, and the world swirled into blackness. I felt my body being moved into a comfortable bed sometime later, and a ticking seemed to be present wherever I was. I tried to tune it out and sleep, but it was ever present.

"Let's leave William to rest and go out to the high tea," The girl said.

"Are you sure that's a good idea? You never know what William could do or where he could go," The boy said.

"If we leave both sides of the door locked, I think he'll be fine," The girl said, "He also looks pretty tired, and a second dose of the medicine should keep him in a restful state for the next few hours,"

"Okay. I'll get his meds," The boy said, "Then we shall go out to tea,"

"Drink this," The girl said, gently nudging my arm to wake me. I obliged, gulping down the horrible tasting green medicine she gave me. It was sour. I laid back onto the bed, and rested in the silence of the room I was in.

ASPEN'S POV (THE HIGH TEA)
Halloween Night, 1860

"I'm so glad we're going to this," I said, exiting our room at the Inn.

"Me too," Fernando said.

We ran down the stairs and made our way into the lobby area and stopped on our way to the table when we both recognized a woman sitting at the table at the exact same time.

"I know you. You fell from the sky in front of my house. I had to call the hospital for you. I never got your names," she said.

"I'm Aspen,"

"I'm Fernando. And you are..,"

"Sophia Hawthorne. Pleased to meet you," she said.

My jaw dropped in disbelief. *Hawthorne.* She wore a large, pink, lacy ball gown with elegant puffy sleeves and a fitted bodice; her hair had been done up in a small bun on the top of her head with ringlets falling down the back of her neck. She wore a necklace with a golden chain and a key at the end. On the handle, an R was engraved on it.

This is the key we've been looking for all this time.

"Nice to meet you too," I said, smiling.

I felt very underdressed compared to how done up Mrs. Hawthorne was.

"Nathaniel should be coming round shortly. He always seems to be running late for these gatherings," Mrs. Hawthorne said.

"Nathaniel as in Nathaniel Hawthorne?" I asked.

"Why, yes my dear," Mrs. Hawthorne said.

"I can't believe this," I whispered to Fernando.

"Me either," he said, back, his eyes sparkling in excitement.

A steady male voice said behind us, "Well if it isn't the children that fell from the heavens,"

We all turned to see a nicely dressed man in a suit and graying hair. He had a handlebar mustache that curled on either side of his lip. He walked towards all of us. Mrs. Hawthorne rose and greeted him with a peck of a kiss on either cheek and a quick hug.

"I'm glad you've finally arrived," Mrs. Hawthorne said.

"I'm looking forward to our high tea," Mr. Hawthorne said.

"I'll catch you up on all the tea," Mrs. Hawthorne said.

"I'm going to get us a pot and a few bites to eat," Mr. Hawthorne said.

When Mr. Hawthorne had arrived back with a hot pot of earl gray tea and an assortment of finger sandwiches, biscuits, and macaroons, we began sipping on the steaming brew and nibbling on the appetizers.

"Why were you late?" Mrs. Hawthorne asked.

"I had a few loose ends to tie up with our wedding and the cruise I'm taking for work after we get married. You'll get to join me after day five for our honeymoon,"

"That sounds marvelous," Mrs. Hawthorne said.

"Wonderful. So, enlighten us on how you fell from the heavens in front of our house. The whole town has been talking about it all day," Mr. Hawthorne said.

"We honestly don't know. We kind of fell through a hole," I said.

"That's rather strange," Mr. Hawthorne said, "Nothing of the sort has ever happened to us before,"

"How's your brother doing?" Mrs. Hawthorne asked.

"Fine," Fernando said.

"He's been sleeping for quite a long time," I said.

"He also unfortunately has minor amnesia," Fernando added solemnly.

"That's terrible," Mrs. Hawthorne said, "If there's anything we can do to help, please let us know,"

"Certainly," Mr. Hawthorne said, taking a bite of a ham and brie finger sandwich.

"Now, I think the two of us should go back up to our room to prepare for our big night pretty soon," Mrs. Hawthorne said.

"What floor are the two of you on?" I asked.

"First floor room eleven," Mrs. Hawthorne said.

"We're on the same floor," I said, "We'll walk with you. We need to check on William anyway,"

When we got back up to the room, we found the door we'd locked on both sides before we'd left wide open, and the bed vacant. William was nowhere to be seen.

As I walked toward the bed, I stepped on something hard, yet squishy at the same time.

"Fernando, look," I said, pointing to the piece of orange peel I had just stepped on. There was a trail leading towards the door.

"We'd better follow this trail and hope it leads us in the right direction," Fernando said, picking up another piece of orange peel near the door.

We headed down the stairs and towards the door of the Inn, I accidentally bumped into Mr. Hawthorne.

"We're so sorry," I said.

"No worries. Where are you kids off to?" He asked.

"Um…. downtown," I said.

"You see, we're not super familiar with this new area, so we're going to go exploring," Fernando said.

"Alright, enjoy," he said.

"How about you?" I asked.

"I'm headed to the port to prepare the sailboat for the cruise I'm taking for work. We need to trade some supplies in the East Indies. Today, we have to load the boat," Mr. Hawthorne said.

"Okay," Fernando said.

Fernando and I pulled on the door to open the Inn, and nothing happened. We pulled again and the door didn't budge.

"Um. Sir, can you please open the door for us to head out?" The hotel manager smiled creepily, with a gap in between his two front teeth and pressed a button that made the door creek slowly open.

"Thanks!" Fernando said.

As we walked down main street the trail of orange peel became longer and longer. Main Street was full of shops, all of which I wanted to go into, but we didn't have the time. *William, where are you?* We followed the trail of orange peel for a while, walking up and down streets, and seemingly passing the same clock shop many times. It was called "Chimes and Co," and from the outside we could hear the dinging, ticking, and tick-tock of many clocks.

"I think we've been walking in circles. This is like the eighth time we've passed this Chimes and Co,"

"Maybe, the clock shop is where we need to go in order to find William,"

I turned the doorknob of the clock shop and was instantly reminded of the Chimes clock room.

"These are too many clocks for me. Too much ticking" I said, covering my ears.

"Same here. I don't see William anywhere," Fernando said, "I feel like I recognize the front desk manager from somewhere though,"

"Let's head to a diner, get a little bite to eat and then keep looking. We have to find him eventually. What does he like to eat or drink? Maybe we can draw him to us with the scent of something he likes to eat,"

"Good idea. He likes Tiramisu," Fernando said.

"Then let's head to the Public House,"

•

"Well hello Aspen and Fernando," Mrs. Hawthorne said as we walked into the diner.

"Hi. How are you?"

"Fine. How about you?" I said.

"Delightful. I'm working on wedding plans. Do you care to join me?"

At the very same time I said, "Yes, please," Fernando said, "No, thanks," We looked at each other.

"One second," I said.

Fernando and I turned our backs on Mrs. Hawthorne.

"So, I'd really love to help with wedding planning, however if you want to stay out of the wedding planning, that's also completely fine," I said.

"Actually, I've just thought of an idea. How about you stay here and help with wedding planning, and I'll buy some tiramisu, keep looking for William and head down to the port to help prepare the boat for the work trip Mr. Hawthorne is about to take. Maybe we can figure out why we tumbled down this rabbit hole from the Hawthornes,"

"Great idea,"

"Mrs. Hawthorne–" I started.

"Oh please, call me Sophia,"

"Sophia, do you think Mr. Hawthorne needs a hand with the boat?" Fernando asked.

"Yes. He can use all the help he can get," Mrs. Hawthorne said. He should be just out of here and to the left. The third sailboat on the right hand side should be his. It's *The Yorkshire,*"

"Okay, that sounds great," Fernando said.

ASPEN AND SOPHIA KATHERINE HAWTHORNE

"By any chance, have you seen William around here anywhere?" I asked.

"No, why?"

"He seems to have wandered away from the hotel. I'm hoping he'll return back tonight,"

"Same here. Isn't it weird that he doesn't remember who you are?"

"Yes, both weird and sad. I want him to trust us," I said.

"I understand,"

"So, you had wedding tasks that needed to be done?"

"Yes, I'd love your help on the invitations and then the wedding cake recipe,"

"That sounds great. I'm so happy for you and Nate," I said.

"I'm so excited for this wedding of ours. It'll be a great day,"

"What date do you have set for the big day?"

"November eleventh,"

"That's just a couple weeks away,"

"Yes, and that's why I need all the help I can get. Here's a pile of invitations. I've done one for you. Here's the list of people we need to send them to. Without further ado, let's get writing,"

"Wait… one question. It says on here to sign it with Sophia K Hawthorne. What does the K stand for?"

"Katherine, my middle name,"

"Oh, I see,"

After about an hour of writing wedding invitations while listening to the soft jazz of the cafe around us my hand cramped from having held the pen for so long.

"I could use a break from wedding invitations," I said.

"Same here. Let's stroll to the town bakery and bake up my wedding cake,"

We both rose, gathered the wedding invitations and headed towards the bakery.

"Sounds great. What's your vision for your wedding cake?"

"I'd like a small chocolate cake for Nate and I to share, and then cupcakes for everyone else,"

"That's a great way to do it," I said, "What flavor of cupcakes are you doing?"

"Pumpkin with cream cheese frosting,"

"Delicious,"

"That means that we have two separate frostings to mix and lots of cake batter to whip up, and this bakery in town only has one oven, so it'll take a while to cook everything,"

"I'm glad. I love the smell of pumpkin muffins," I said.

"While the wonderful smell wafts over to us in the kitchen, how about we finish the wedding invitations, and then I'll have you run them to the post office for me,"

When we arrived at the bakery, we headed to the back kitchen.

"Here's the recipe for the chocolate cake. Be sure to follow it precisely," Mrs. Hawthorne said.

"I will," I promised, "May I ask how Nate proposed to you?"

"Why, of course!" Mrs. Hawthorne said, as she began gathering ingredients for the pumpkin cupcakes.

"It was New Year's Day when he proposed to me. He and I had a romantic dinner date planned for New Years Eve, and after our dinner date we planned on heading back to his house. The dinner was at Rockafellas. I had spaghetti and meatballs, and he had a shrimp and rice dish. The conversation over our meal was positive and I felt happy to be with him. As we walked down the streets of Salem, MA after our meal,

I noticed we weren't heading back towards his house. When I asked him where we were going, he said, "You'll see," We passed many shops and cemeteries, until we finally reached our destination: A garden. This garden wasn't any garden though. It was the garden where we had first met. It was located on the right hand side of a white Ropes Mansion. The Jasmine growing on the arch trellis as we went into the garden was fragrant. He pulled me close for a hug and whispered in my ear, "I love you," Then, he got down on one knee as the fairy lights all around the garden came on and we began to hear fireworks in the distance. He said, "Sophia, I have loved you for a long time. Ever since the moment I first met you when Abigail introduced you to me and I instantly became infatuated with you: you have been there for me too. I'd be the happiest man on earth if you'd agree to be my wife and spend the rest of your life with me. Sophia Katherine Hawthorne, will you marry me?" I of course said yes and then he kissed me, and we stayed the night at his house,"

"That sounds like the dreamiest night ever," I said.

"I know, right," Mrs. Hawthorne said, her eyes sparkling.

I began mixing the butter, eggs, milk, and brown sugar for the chocolate cake. In the dry ingredient bowl, I added cocoa powder, flour, baking soda and salt. After mixing the dry and wet ingredients together, I poured the batter into a circular loaf pan.

"Can I taste your batter?" I asked.

"Yes," Mrs. Hawthorne said, handing me her spatula.

I sighed because it tasted delicious.

"You're a great cook. This is so good," I said.

"Thanks!"

"Where is your sister by the way?" I asked.

"I honestly don't know. She's probably wandering around town doing something,"

"You're not close, I'm guessing," I said, as I put the cake into the oven.

"No, we're polar opposites. We don't tend to like to spend a lot of time together. And she always seems to be off doing things in town. She'll never tell me what she's out doing,"

"That sounds like it would be annoying," I said.

"Yes, it is. And she never tells our parents where she's going in town either,"

"That's a bit sketchy,"

"Yes,"

I began washing all the dishes in the sink and placing them on the drying rack. Mrs. Hawthorne had all the pumpkin cupcakes ready to be cooked, so we sat down at the table in the kitchen and relaxed for a little bit until the cake needed to be frosted and the next batch of pumpkin muffins needed to go into the oven.

"Time to make some frosting," Mrs. Hawthorne said.

"Did you want cream cheese for the pumpkin cupcakes and vanilla for the chocolate cake?" I asked.

"Yes,"

"Can we do a vanilla cream cheese frosting with the chocolate double layer cake?" I asked.

"Marvelous idea. Please, help yourself to all the cream cheese and powdered sugar you need," Mrs. Hawthorne said.

"Can you please grab me the mixer?" I asked.

"On it,"

After we had mixed the frostings together, and the cake had fully cooled, we frosted the chocolate cake and decorated the top with white edible flours made from the frosting.

"This looks beautiful," I said.

"Just wait until we decorate the cupcakes," Mrs. Hawthorne replied.

"I'm excited to see how pretty they turn out,"

After we had finished all the baking and frosting, we headed back to the Inn for the night. Then, I got ready for bed and noticed that Sophia was sitting at the desk writing on a piece of parchment paper. The quill made large swipes up and down on the page as she wrote in loopy cursive. Her eyebrows knitted together as if deep in concentration.

"What are you writing about?" I asked.

"Nothing," she said, a small smile growing on her face.

"You've got to be writing about something interesting. I can tell from your grin,"

"I'm writing to my future husband,"

"Oh,"

"I'm writing about everything," She said dreamily.

She seemed to stare off into space as she answered my question. Many peaceful memories seemed to rest on her spirit as she wrote more. The curiosity about the words on the page blossomed in my mind. I wondered what specifically she was writing about and why she chose here to write the letters. Maybe Salem, MA called the dreamer inside her to write about the many dreams she had during their marriage and honeymoon. Maybe a time away from Nate helped her see things in a new light and the thoughts were so strong and clear that they demanded to be written on the pages.

"Where do you plan on getting married?" I asked into the silence of the room.

"Boston, Massachusetts,"

"I love the Boston area," I said, "How did you pick Boston?"

"It's near the ports that we're going to be heading out of for our honeymoon, and it's convenient for Nate's business trip arrival home," She answered, seeming slightly annoyed.

"One more question and then I'll let you write more,"

"And that is?" She said, tapping her fingers on the desk.

"When are Nate and Fernando supposed to be back from the port?" I asked.

"That's a very good question. I don't know,"

"You're not worried about them, are you?"

"I'm a little worried, but I know Nate knows his way around town and sometimes loading the boat is a rather lengthy process,"

"Okay. I'm hoping they get back soon," I said, sleepily.

I yawned, and my eyelids began to feel heavy. The last thing I remembered before falling asleep was a clock sitting on the desk with a golden logo on it which I recognized from *Chimes and Co* imprinted onto the bottom right corner of the wooden clock stand. When I awoke the next morning, the clock dinged at nine and then the outline of the clock grew bigger and bigger until golden stands of magic pulled me into time.

FERNANDO
Early Afternoon, After Meeting at the Coffee Shop

"William. William," I called every few steps, "I have tiramisu for you,"

No answer. People began to stare at me as I continued walking. I looked away from them, slightly embarrassed.

This is ridiculous. You're calling out your brother's name as if he was a dog. He's not a dog. Where is he? Why can't I find him?

I continued to walk and eat my tiramisu.

I'm hoping William is found soon. Usually, he doesn't run off like this when he sleepwalks. This past week has been the worst cases of sleepwalking and nightmares I've ever seen. I wish he could finally find peace and for more than just one night, so we could stop searching for him and be happy. I want to feel content with life's circumstances, but life's circumstances are constantly changing. I have to adapt and focus on what I can control.

"William," I called again, one more time growing scared and frustrated.

No answer.

I wondered if the worst had happened to him and my vision blurred around me. When I blinked and a tear rolled down my cheek, I saw a crow above me drop a piece of parchment paper at my feet and fly away without so much as a *caw* in greeting. The parchment paper was tied in a bow with a red ribbon. I undid the bow and unrolled the parchment paper.

Dear Fernando,

Sometimes there are random detours in life that add to the enrichment of your journey as a whole. You'll be challenged though these detours and in time, they will lead you back to the right path. There is a detour coming to you in the near future. Trust the universe and your intuition and you will find your brother.

Sincerely,

Mr. C

I felt as though helping Mr. Hawthorne load the boat would ultimately lead me to where I needed to go and I could only hope that it would lead me back to my brother eventually, in time.

After walking for a little while I arrived at the boat ramp and spotted a girl dressed in an all-black long sleeve dress from head to toe.

"Hi," I said.

"Hi. Do you know if I can get onto these boats without a ticket?" She asked.

"I think you can. Let me go ask," I said, "Follow me,"

The girl followed me down the ramp towards Mr. Hawthorne's boat.

"Mr. Hawthorne," I said, "Do you need to buy a ticket to come onto the boats?"

"No. Why do you ask?"

"I was wondering if she could come help us with loading the boat," I said, nodding towards the girl who politely stood next to me.

"Yeah, sure. We need all the help we can get,"

"Mr. Hawthorne. What do you need us to do?" I asked, after we had entered the boat.

"First, please call me Nate. Mr. Hawthorne is a mouthful," He said, "Secondly, please go to the boat supply center and bring as many boxes of earl gray tea as you can. We need to ship it out of here soon,"

"Okay," I said.

"We're on it," The girl said, tucking a stray strand of black hair behind her ear.

"I'm sorry. I never introduced myself," I said as we walked out of the boat and onto the ramp.

"I'm Fernando. Nice to meet you,"

"I'm Abigail," The girl said.

I really wanted to ask her if she was hot in her dress because if I were her, I'd be sweating buckets. Instead, I decided to keep my mouth shut. It was a warm day outside, possibly in the mid eighties, and the sea breeze blew as we walked around near the water. I smelled a hint of salt in the air as we continued to walk.

"What brings you to Salem today?" I asked.

"I needed some time to think," she said, tucking her hair behind her ear once again as the breeze blew it all around her face. She blushed slightly, but it went away again almost instantly.

"This wind is no joke," I said, as we arrived at the boat supply building.

"You're very right,"

I opened the door to reveal piles upon piles of boxes of earl gray tea.

"This is going to take a while," I said, sighing loudly.

"Indeed," Abigail said.

"I wonder if Mr. Hawthorne has a cart to pull these boxes back and forth,"

"That would be enormously helpful,"

We each grabbed a heavy box of Earl Gray tea from the supply closet and headed back to the Luxury passenger ship.

"Nate," I said.

"Yeah," he said, unrolling his white sails.

"Do you have a cart to move these back and forth?" I asked.

"Nope. It all needs to be done by hand. The nearest log cart would be one pulled by a mule and they should be working the land instead of working here," Nate said, "Can one of you help me tie up one of these sails?"

"Yes," Abigail said.

"I'll go grab another box of tea,"

When I arrived back at the boat carrying a large box of tea, Abigail had tied up one sail and was helping Mr. Hawthorne with the other one.

"You have to tie it tight, Abigail. Otherwise, the boat won't sail as fast as we need it to," Mr. Hawthorne said.

"Like this?"

"Yes, but way tighter. Also, you need to zigzag the ties as if you're making a figure eight. That tie is closer to a square than zigzag,"

"Okay. I'll try again,"

When I arrived back with a third box of tea, Abigail had finished tying the second sail.

"Is this right?" She asked.

"Yes. Great job," Mr. Hawthorne said.

"Thank you. I'm going to use the bathroom. Does this ship have plumbing?" Abigail asked.

"Yes," Mr. Hawthorne said.

"How many boxes of tea do you need and where do they ultimately need to go?" I asked.

"Let me show you," Mr. Hawthorne said.

Mr. Hawthorne led me down a steep winding staircase at the starboard side of the ship near the wheel. He opened a trap door to reveal the staircase and took each step very carefully down to the bottom deck. When we finally arrived at the bottom deck, I saw a big sign on the wall that read *Storage*.

"Does all the tea ultimately go underneath the storage sign?" I asked.

"Yes. That would be correct. I want to show you one more thing," he said, continuing to walk through the lower floor.

"Here's where the sailors sleep," he said, showing me a hallway of dormitory sized rooms each with a number on the door. The right-hand side door started at one and progressively went up as we walked down the hallway. The left hand side door ended at forty.

"Do you really have forty crew members?" I asked, shocked at how many people would be riding *The Yorkshire*.

"Yes, plus more people to help with the loading and unloading. You included, but we don't leave until tomorrow night, a few days before the big wedding day,"

"Wow. Are you getting excited about the wedding?" I asked.

"Yes. I'm cautiously excited because it'll be a busy time for us as always,"

"Definitely. Sometimes being busy is fun,"

"Very true. You're wise for your age," Mr. Hawthorne said.

"Thank you. Where will I be sleeping?" I asked.

"Room number twelve,"

"Sounds great,"

As we headed back upstairs and rounded the corner, we found Abigail standing at the top of the steep staircase looking very lost once again.

"I can't seem to find the bathroom," she said,

"It's down here," Mr. Hawthorne said.

"Oh," she said, embarrassed.

"Be careful as you're coming down," Mr. Hawthorne coached her.

"Will do," she said, gripping the railing and taking one step at a time.

As Mr. Hawthorne showed Abigail to the bathroom, I headed back to the cargo storage and grabbed another box of tea to carry back to the ship. I thought that it might be best to start moving the tea down to the storage area before letting it pile up on the main deck. As I carried a box of tea down to the bottom deck, a guilty-looking Abigail looked back at me.

"How are you?" I asked.

"Good," she said, her voice going up a couple notches. She tucked her hair behind her ear again. Her "good" sounded more like a question than a reply. I wanted to know what she wasn't telling me. What wasn't good?

"And you?" She asked.

"I'm starting to get tired," I said.

"I can help with a few more boxes," Abigail said, "Then I need to get going,"

"Where are you off to next?" I asked.

"Supper at Rockafellas,"

"That sounds fun," I said, "What do you think you're going to order?"

"I don't know yet. Maybe stew?"

"Okay. I'll hand you boxes of tea. If you could put the boxes near the first one, that would be great. Then, I'll go get the rest," I said.

"That sounds great. When you leave to get the rest of the boxes, I'll head to supper,"

"Okay,"

After about five boxes had been transported to the lower level, Abigail came back up and said goodbye to Mr. Hawthorne. We walked down the ramp together and when we had reached the end, I said, "Bye. It was nice meeting you Abigail,"

"Nice meeting you too. Bye. I might see you around?"

"Maybe," I said, shrugging.

I walked to the storage center and grabbed another box of tea and headed back to Mr. Hawthorne.

"Quirky girl," Nate said as soon as I got back.

"Yes, very. Have you ever met her before?" I asked.

"Nope,"

"Why did you let her on your boat?"

"Same reason why I let you on the boat. I need all the help I can get,"

"Makes sense," I said hesitantly, "What have you been busy doing?"

"Planning the trip and organizing everything on the upper deck. I need to do the pre-sailing checks tonight, so we can head out in the morning,"

"Sounds interesting," I said, "Can I see what you have mapped out for the trip?"

"Yeah, sure. The round trip takes about three days and three nights, and it could take longer depending on the amount of wind we get there and back. Weather plays a huge role in our luck with this trip,"

"That makes sense,"

Mr. Hawthorne pulled out his map of the seas.

"Here's our route," he said as he pointed to a blue line.

"And here's a similar, yet longer route with the same destination," he said, as he pointed to a red line.

"It looks like it's important to always have backups," I said, pointing to all the additional lines he had added on the map other than the first two.

"That's a sailing strategy. Anything could happen out at sea. The weather could be bad, and we could have to reroute towards sunny skies and somehow navigate around the bad weather to the same destination,"

"That's why we have Google maps," I said, not thinking before speaking. I instantly covered my mouth after the words had slipped out.

"What is Google maps?" Nate asked, slightly confused.

"Nothing. It's not around yet. Pretend you never heard that," I said.

"Okay. I mean... I know what maps are........ Hmm. But what's Google?" He asked.

"No need to know quite yet. You'll know eventually," I said.

"I see how it is. You like to keep secrets," he said, winking.

"Maybe it's for the greater good,"

"Okay. Then, I'll wait and see what this Google thing is," he said, smiling.

"In the meantime, what other pre-sailing checks do you need to do?" I asked.

"I need to check the food supply, plumbing, water supply, and stock the boat with everything we're trading,"

"I'll bring over some more boxes of tea then," I said.

The sky had turned a gentle shade of pink, and cotton candy orange. *Wow. It's sunset already? That time flew by.*

I carried about a half dozen boxes onto the ship before the sun sank the rest of the way into the horizon.

"Do you think we should pause loading the ship until tomorrow morning?" I asked.

"Yes. I'd like you to make the beds for all the crew members living on this ship though, and double check the plumbing in the bathroom," Mr. Hawthorne said.

I nodded.

"After you're done with that, we'll head back to the Inn, and wake before dawn tomorrow morning to finish loading this ship. The rest of the crew will be here tomorrow as well to help,"

"You know what?" I asked.

"What?" Mr. Hawthorne asked.

"I've been thinking you've been working hard all day, and you should head back to the Inn a little early today. I'll finish up around here and meet you back at the Inn when I'm done,"

"Are you sure?"

"Yes," I said confidently.

"Thank you so much. I appreciate your hard work," Mr. Hawthorne said.

"You're welcome,"

I double checked the plumbing first because something about the way Abigail had looked extremely guilty when she came out of the bathroom didn't sit well with me. Something was up. Something caused her to look guilty.

I opened the bathroom door to see all the normal things: a toilet, a sink, and a shower. The smell of the bathroom was repulsive. It smelled like rotten eggs. I held my nose as I opened the cabinet underneath the sink to look at the pipes. I tried to wiggle them, and they stayed solid in place. I opened the toilet seat and saw that Abigail had never flushed. I held the flush button down and it cleared Abigails waste. Yet, the rotten egg smell still lingered.

I decided to start making the forty beds for the crew members. The sheets had been delivered to the rooms, and I started making every bed, with the sheets pulled all the way up. It seemed to take forever to get all the sheets on and the beds ready, but eventually every bed had been made, and I headed back up to the main deck.

"Did you by chance smell a rotten egg smell from the bathroom when you were down there earlier?" I asked Mr. Hawthorne.

"No. Let me check it again, though," he said.

I opened the trap door for him, and he took one step at a time all the way down towards the lower deck. He looked down at his watch when he stood at the bottom of the staircase.

"Holy moly. It's eleven at night already?" he said, shocked.

"Wow. That's late. Totally lost track of time," I said.

"We should head back to the Inn ASAP. Sophia will be expecting me,"

I opened the bathroom door, and he sniffed the air.

"I don't smell it," he said.

"Go in further," I said.

He walked into the bathroom and said, "I still don't smell

anything out of the ordinary,"

"Really?" I said, "I could have sworn it smelled strongly of rotten eggs earlier,"

"It might have. But, while you were making the beds, the scent must have cleared out. We'll keep an eye on it,"

"Great idea,"

"I'll light a lantern, and we'll walk back to the Inn. I hope we get there before midnight," Nate said.

"I'm exhausted," I said.

As we walked back, there was a slight chill in the air on the breeze that rustled the trees above us. I shivered as goosebumps trickled down my spine. The whole town of Salem seemed to be sleeping. The streets were quiet with the occasional buggy, or carriage every now and then but other than that there was silence. The streetlights were lit and illuminated our path back to the Inn.

The butler greeted us and held the door for us as we walked in through the heavy wooden doors of the Inn. An older man sat at the front desk with a sleeping cap and a white beard. We nodded to him as we headed up to our rooms. He nodded back and looked about ready to fall asleep but forced himself to keep his eyes open.

I knocked on the door of the room I was supposed to be staying in. Aspen opened the door slowly and groggily. She said, "Welcome back" and started walking back to bed. She climbed into bed and went back to sleep.

"Hi. I'm so happy you're back," Sophia said, as she embraced Nate.

"I'm happy to be back. Sorry it's so late,"

"No problem,"

"Fernando, we're in the room next to yours. Meet me at five in the morning tomorrow to finish loading the ship," Mr. Hawthorne said.

"Will do," I said.

Nate grabbed Sophia's hand and they walked down the hallway together.

"What have you been busy doing?" Nate asked in a hushed whisper.

"Writing," Sophia said, and they disappeared into the room next to ours.

I could hear their muffled chatter as they continued to talk in their room. I looked towards the wall that backed up to their room and saw why. We had adjoining rooms connected by a door with an illuminated keyhole.

I know I shouldn't intrude on their privacy but I'm so curious to know what they're doing and talking about.

Ultimately, my curiosity won, and I slowly pressed my eye towards the keyhole and watched them. They held each other in an embrace for a while, only whispering words to each other which I couldn't hear. The way in which they held each other as if their significant other was the most precious thing on earth left me in awe of their story. They pulled apart and Sophia asked, "How did the ship prep go?"

"Pretty well. I met an interesting little girl though,"

"Why was she interesting?"

"For starters, her clothing was all black, and long sleeve,"

"That sounds extremely hot,"

"Agreed. How did wedding preparations go over here?"

"Extremely well,"

"Good. I'm happy to hear that. Now, will you finally tell me what you've been writing about? I'm dying to know,"

"Not yet,"

"Please?" Nate begged, giving Sophia puppy eyes.

"On our wedding day. You'll read every single letter I've ever written to you,"

"Okay," Nate said, giving Sophia a mock frowny face.

"I just need you to promise me that you'll be safe out on the waters," Sophia blurted out.

"Why do you say that?"

"Well…. You know anything can happen out there,"

"I promise to be safe out there and get home safely so I can marry you and we can have our honeymoon together. I love you so much,"

Sophia and Nate had moved to sitting on the edge of the bed and Nate tucked a stray strand of hair behind Sophia's ear.

"I love you too," Sophia said.

"Well. I guess I'd better get some rest before the big day tomorrow," Nate said, flipping the light switch.

"Me too. We still have some cupcakes to make and frost. Having one oven to work with is not recommended,"

"Makes sense. Good night. Even in the darkness of this bedroom, you shine with the light that of a dove,"

"Thank you. Sleep well. Sweet dreams,"

"My dreams will be very sweet, my darling,"

They fell asleep holding each other and I was asleep on the other side of the door minutes after.

•

The next morning, I awoke to the gentle tap on my shoulder from Mr. Hawthorne.

"It's time to head down for breakfast," Mr. Hawthorne whispered.

"Okay," I said, although I still felt sluggish and disinterested in going down for breakfast, but I knew I had to.

After I was dressed and ready for the day, I headed down to the breakfast buffet in the lobby. I saw the word coffee written on a cylinder-shaped large bottle dispenser and immediately headed towards it.

"You like coffee, huh?" Mr. Hawthorne asked.

"Yes, with hot cocoa powder," I said.

"I like it black,"

"It's not too bitter to your taste?" I asked.

"No, after a while you get used to it,"

"What time are we aiming to leave the port this morning?" I asked as we made our way through the breakfast buffet.

"Eight. If we leave later. It'll be okay too,"

I filled my plate with two egg omelets, a bagel and a fruit salad. Nate filled his with two pieces of toast, two hard boiled eggs and some smeared avocado on his toast. He grabbed a banana as well before sitting down to eat. We chatted over breakfast about upcoming wedding plans for Nate and what he thought the next few days would bring. After we had finished breakfast, we headed back upstairs to gather our belongings and say our goodbyes.

"Bye Aspen," I said, as I gave her a quick friendly hug.

"I need you to meet me at Chimes and Co when you get back. It's a rabbit hole," She whispered in my ear.

"Will do," I said, as I followed Mr. Hawthorne down the hallway of the Inn and out the front door.

We walked briskly to the boat and joined the rest of the crew. My arm muscles ached as I grabbed what felt like the thousandth box of earl gray tea and brought it back onto the boat. I paused for a moment as I watched the white and grey seagulls flying around the boat and marveled at the sounds they made as they flew. I watched them flying near the water and listened to the sound of the waves lapping against the boat. The salty sea breeze that blew my short hair around felt welcoming, and exhilarating. I had that feeling of exuberance when you're about to go somewhere. The thrill of excitement that rested within my tired body was enough to keep me going throughout the morning.

I didn't know what the next few days would hold, but I did know that they would be interesting because this was my first sailboat ride ever. I put a little bit more pep in my step as I loaded the last few boxes with the help of the rest of the crew.

"Nate," I said, as I walked up to him. He was standing on the starboard side of the ship in front of the steering wheel, looking through his binoculars. I followed his gaze to the beautiful sunrise on the horizon. The sky was full of puffy clouds that looked like cotton balls. They were all different shades of cotton candy pink and orange.

"Yes,"

"I believe all the boxes of tea are loaded,"

"That's great. To confirm, there are no more boxes of tea left at the storage bin by the docks,"

"Yes, that's correct. They're all here on the lower deck,"

"Great. I'll go let everyone know we're leaving. I think most of the crew reported this morning though,"

"All aboard," Nate called to the people walking by.

They simply shook their heads and kept walking down the street.

"It looks like we can go," I said.

"Can you untie the figure eights Abigail tied yesterday, please?"

"Yes. I'm on it,"

We pushed off the dock at five after eight in the morning and headed towards Norfolk with our ultimate destination being the East Indies to trade the earl gray tea and arrive back before the wedding. I still felt exhausted from the lack of sleep from the night before, so I headed down to the bottom deck to get some rest. When I opened my room, I noticed a blue suitcase waiting for me on the bed. There was a white tag on the handle which read:

Everything you'll need for the next few days.

- *Mr. C*

I unzipped the suitcase to find a couple folded pants, shirts, and underclothes on the right side. On the other side was an assortment of clocks. *Why is this man obsessed with so many clocks?* The clocks included a pocket watch that looked almost identical to Mr. Chime's, an alarm clock, a mini co-co clock, and a mini grandfather clock. *No one in their right mind would take four clocks on vacation. That's ridiculous.*

I placed the alarm clock on the bedside table and calibrated it to the day and time. While I was calibrating it, I found tight cursive writing engraved on the bottom right side of the clock. It read *Psalm 4:9*. I sat the clock on the bedside table and rested peacefully.

•

Sometime later, I was jolted awake by Mr. Hawthorne. His eyes were filled with worry, fear, and terror. It was nighttime, and the boat sounded of many hurried footsteps up and down the hallway.

"What happened?" I asked.

"I need to show you something," he said, urgently.

I crawled out of bed and the boat seemed to rock underneath my feet. The walls of the ship seemed to creak and moan as we walked through the hallway to what Mr. Hawthorne had to show me. As we walked, he said, "I feel bad for not looking further into that rotten egg smell,"

He opened the bathroom door on the lower deck for an instant to show a stream of water shooting towards the door from the pipes underneath the sink.

"Our plumbing is all messed up. If that pipe breaks fully, we can't do dishes, or use that bathroom at all, and besides our safety is up in the air right now," Mr. Hawthorne said.

"You mean, if we don't fix this broken pipe in the bathroom, we could sink before we return back to the dock?"

"Yes. That's why all these crew members have been alerting everyone. We're trying to get as many people off the ship as possible. I don't know how much time we have," He said, apprehensively.

"I'll work on fixing the pipe," I said.

"Don't bother, we have plumbers coming in to help with it in a few minutes. I need you at the starboard side steering the ship in the night. The wind has significantly died down, and if we don't get any wind tonight, we'll probably be behind on the delivery date for the earl gray tea,"

"What happens if it doesn't arrive at the port or we can't make it there?"

"Then, we let off the red flair to indicate, we're slowly sinking,"

"What if nobody sees it?" I asked.

"Then, we're stranded,"

"Can you swim?"

"Yes. Can you?"

"Yes,"

"The water temperature today before we left was 35 degrees Fahrenheit,"

"That's frigid,"

"Exactly. I don't know if we can survive the chill,"

"I see,"

"My guess is that we have two days tops until the boat sinks,"

"Okay," I said, nodding.

Inside my heart, I knew the pain Mr. Hawthorne must be feeling. He probably felt grief over the wedding that might not happen because he might never make it back, due to this broken pipe and a lack of concern for the plumbing system.

"Where are your maps?" I asked.

"Captain's chambers, directly underneath the wheel," Mr. Hawthorne said, "Here's the key,"

Mr. Hawthorne took off his gold chain necklace, a golden key hung at the bottom. The golden key had a circular loop at one end which the chain went through, and some cursive scribbled on the long side that was too small for me to read. There were two spokes that came down from the long side of the key.

"We're on the blue route?" I asked.

"Yes. Hurry up now. I'm going to try to get some rest and switch out with you in the morning,"

I walked down to the captain's room and inserted the spokes at the end of the long key into the door. It creaked open and I walked over to the desk. On top of the desk sat a piece of parchment paper addressed to Miss Sophia Katherine Hawthorne with about a half of a page written in tight, neat cursive. Next to the cursive page sat the charts. I picked up the pile of maps. From just outside the room, I heard a loud creak and moan of the pipes. The rotten egg smell was spreading to other parts of the ship.

I locked the door and walked back up to the starboard side of the ship. *What could Mr. Hawthorne have been writing about? I thought that only Sophia was writing letters to her fiancé? Maybe Nate just doesn't want Sophia to know about the letters just yet.*

I steered the ship by candlelight and got little to no wind. The creaking of the boat whenever the wind did pick up made me feel as if the boat was coming alive. The candlelight cast a shadow around the captain's chamber of the boat as candlewax dripped down the side of the candle. The tiny lights were reflected in the dark, murky, waters that made me feel squeamish inside. We were floating extremely slowly by the current downstream. The evening chill gave me goosebumps as I stared into the starry night sky reflecting off the clear water. Eventually, I tried to relax into the silence of the gentle sea air as it tickled my skin as the boat rocked back and forth in a rhythmic motion. It became more and more difficult to be scared as the rocking of the boat became more frequent and soothing. I slowly forgot about everything there was to be concerned about and thought about resting my eyes for a few seconds.

No, Mr. Hawthorne is counting on you to steer this ship. You must stay awake.

Even though steering was extremely boring as the next few hours ticked by, I stayed awake. The creaks and moans of the pipes were the only sound on the ship followed by the hushed whispers of some of the passengers and crew on the main deck. Eventually, around six in the morning, the day began to break across the horizon. The sun made its appearance across the cloud-filled sky. The sun was an orangey-red hue as it rose into the blue sky. The sun reflected in the water leaving me in awe of the natural beauty around me.

"It's beautiful, isn't it?" said a voice behind me.

"Yes," I said, turning around to face Mr. Hawthorne who looked on edge. From the bags underneath his eyes, I could tell he hadn't slept all night.

"I need to show you something in case the worst-case scenario comes true,"

"Okay," I said, following him down a flight of stairs to the captain's room.

"Of all my voyages aboard this ship, I have by far spent most of my time in this room," He said, "I have touched quill to parchment many times within this room, writing about my many voyages and to the many people I love most in this world,"

"Like Sophia?" I asked.

"Yes, exactly. I have also spent loads of time in between steering this ship and doing maintenance on the ship writing to my own family about the weather conditions, boat conditions and onward. All those letters to family members have been sent," Mr. Hawthorne said.

"But Sophia is special," I said, guessing where he was going with his ramblings.

"Yes, extremely special. My intention was to give her the letters I've written to her during our time apart from each other on our wedding night. And now –" His voice cracked as the raw truth sunk in.

I might not survive until the wedding day. My mind finished the sentence for him.

Silence hung over us as he took a moment to collect himself again.

"The bottom of the boat is starting to fill with water," He finished, "The plumbers can't do much to fix that, so we're officially sinking! I can't believe this is happening,"
I looked up to his face and saw the sadness, terror, anger, and grief in his eyes as a tear started rolling down his cheek.

"I'm so sorry," I said, sympathetically.

"No need to be sorry. It's all my fault. I wish I could realistically say I could get back safely but we didn't have enough rowboats for all the passengers and all the rowboats have already been used. And that's where you come in," Mr. Hawthorne said, his voice cracking with emotion, "I need you to carry on my legacy,"

"How?" I asked.

"With this," Mr. Hawthorne said, presenting me with another key, "I think you know what this unlocks,"

This key had a golden clock engraved on the handle. The hour hand pointed at nine and the minute hand pointed at twelve. *Patience* was the word engraved on the long rod of the key. I looked at the key and looked back up at Mr. Hawthorne. Behind him, my eyes found a locked safe behind his desk. The lock was heart shaped and seemed to tick as if it was a clock. I nodded towards the safe and Mr. Hawthorne nodded.

"Patience," He reminded me, "Nine at night,"
I nodded.

Somehow Mr. Hawthorne knew I would make it out of this boat alive and back to the future safely. It almost felt creepy that he knew where I would be in just a few more hours and when I would be. *He's not related to you, is he?* The thought seemed to float around in my mind for most of the morning as I helped more passengers up to the main deck.

By around noon, the wooden boards on the bottom of the boat had begun to break. I saw the plumbers come up from the bottom deck soaked and shivering. I grabbed the flare gun from a cabinet below the captain's seat and shot a red flare into the sky in hopes that people would see it and come to rescue at least some of us. Nate steered the boat and continued to operate the boat calmly as if nothing was happening.

A man stood, praying on the boat. Another woman stood on the top deck with her child pulled in close to her chest. *We only have a matter of time.* I felt the boat slowly begin to get heavier as the wood cracked more.

My guess was that we had a few more hours before the whole boat capsized.

"Everyone, grab a life jacket and get in a lifeboat. We're sinking," Mr. Hawthorne yelled at passengers near us.

I handed out lifejackets to frightened-looking passengers. Everyone rushed around me in a flurry of activity, panicking. Some were saying their last goodbyes before being put on separate lifeboats. Others were rushing around trying to get to a lifeboat as fast as possible. A woman nearby me was crying. The man next to her was in a stunned state of shock, frozen in fear.

"Here. Hurry. Get into a lifeboat," I said, my handing them a life jacket as I heard another crack. The man snapped out of his shock, and the woman dabbed tears from her cheeks as she took the lifejacket from me and rushed to a lifeboat.

Another family nearby hugged me as they said their goodbyes before climbing into separate lifeboats. I handed a life jacket to each of them and knew I needed to carry out my promise to Mr. Hawthorne and time was fleeting.

I rushed around to the other side of the boat and saw where the crack had come from – the stern. It was almost totally submerged in water. I decided it was time to gather the last possessions I needed as time was slipping away. I grabbed the floating alarm clock from the lower deck and decided I needed to open the safe early, otherwise it wouldn't contain What *if the key goes to multiple locks?* The ticking seemed to stop as I heard a loud crack. *Oh shoot.*

"Abandon ship," Mr. Hawthorne yelled to all the crew members, scurrying around in terror.

The lock clicked and the door opened wide. Inside sat a shoebox covered with blue wrapping paper. On the side of the box Nate had written: *To my dearest Sophia.* I grabbed the box and started to tinker with the alarm clock. If the lock didn't need to be set to nine in the morning to unlock, then the alarm clock probably needed to be set to the correct time for me to escape the boat.

Bullhorns blared in the distance.

"We are abandoning the ship!" Crew members yelled.

Mr. Hawthorne gave me one last look with his eyes full of hope amidst the grief I'm sure hovered over him. I nodded at him as if saying: *I'll make sure your Sophia knows how much you love her.* He wore his heavy black sailing boots and a tri-corner sailing hat as he walked the plank and disappeared into the sea below.

The clock had been set to nine am. I tapped it twice before opening up the glass outside covering the numbers and hands on the clock. The golden rays of magic streamed out from the clock and pulled me into a whirlwind of numbers, letters, and sounds from clocks until I crash landed in the middle of the woods, completely disoriented as to where I was. It was entirely dark outside, and I heard a wolf howling in the distance. *Oh great! I'd better not get eaten alive out here. I was supposed to meet Aspen at Chimes and Co. Why did the rabbit hole drop me here?*

FERNANDO

1860 Grandma's house

I looked around at everything around me. As my eyes adjusted, I recognized this path as somewhere I'd been before. I was at the bottom of a trail that was at the bottom of a mountain. The fallen tree to my right confirmed my suspicions. I walked briskly up the trail to the blue house at the top of the mountain. Every switchback up the path meant I was getting ever closer to my final destination. My heart pounded in my chest as I knew I was here at this house for a reason. I knew Mr. Chimes wouldn't drop me here for no reason.

The blue house finally came into view and a fire was lit in the fireplace as smoke was coming out of the chimney. I felt the cool breeze on my skin as I walked up the stairs to the front porch. The door knocker, this time didn't have the same face as before. Instead of Aspen's grandmother's face, there was the face of the pale girl I had met on the boat ramp. Her black hair was straight, and her right eye was closed as if winking at me. *Well, that's creepy.*
I lifted the door knocker ring only to lift it out of her mouth. I jumped back in surprise as the mouth started talking to me.

"Who are you?" It asked.

"Fernando," I squeaked out.

"I need you to come in," it said as the wooden door creaked open revealing a darkened cabin except for the fire lit in the fireplace.

The cabin was silent for a few minutes other than the crackling in the fireplace. I also felt like I heard someone breathing deeply but couldn't be sure.

"Hello?" I said.

Someone tapped me on the shoulder as I took another step forward. I turned around, and from the little bit I could see from the firelight, she looked almost identical to the girl at the boat, just slightly older.

"Hi Fernando," The deep female voice said.

"Who are you?" I asked, goosebumps prickling up my spine. Something inside of me didn't want to trust her.

"Abigail,"

That's exactly who I thought she was.

"And what do you want from me?" I asked.

"I want you to have tea," she said. Her voice seemed to echo throughout the house.

"No, thanks," I said, trying to walk up the stairs.

Not so fast! The chilly breeze on my shoulder whispered in my ear.

"You will be doing no such thing," Abigail said, blocking the stairs.

I heard a snoring coming from a room upstairs that sounded eerily familiar.

"William! William!" I called up the stairs.

Abigail's icy fingertips covered my mouth. She held me from behind and whispered in my ear, "He won't wake yet. He's in a deep slumber, so you must sit down and tell me everything,"

The hesitation I felt to trust Abigail was undeniable. I absolutely despised how she had such a clever way of getting to me and making me do whatever she wanted. I sat on the comfy looking chair by the fireplace and Abigail sat across from me.

"You must answer all my questions, otherwise you'll end up with all the people upstairs. Or worse – the people outside," she said as she raised the blinds.

The window revealed a large graveyard with many illumined gravestones under the full moon.

I thought I heard the stomping upstairs of heavy boots, but it was so faint that I couldn't be sure.

"First, what is this box you have?" She asked.

"Nothing you need to be concerned about,"

"Oh come on. I know you're not telling me something. Spill," She commanded.

The debate in my head between telling her they were Nathaniel Hawthorne's letters to Sophia or lying to her and dancing around the truth stretched the silence longer and longer.

"Spit it out. Any day now," she said, tapping her foot on the ground.

"It's letters," I finally blurted out.

Water seemed to be gushing through the pipes from upstairs.

"I'll be right back. STAY!" Abigail said.

"My plumbing is so bad," Abigail muttered under her breath as she climbed the stairs.

As soon as she was out of sight, I bolted towards the door. I needed to find Aspen and William. I pulled on the door handle. Locked.

Not so fast. The icy breeze seemed to whisper in my ear once again. Abigail had somehow snuck up behind me and pulled me away from the door with her fingers which were ice cold. The heavy boot steps continued upstairs. They grew louder and louder until they stopped.

"Let me go," I yelled at Abigail.

I need to get upstairs and rescue William somehow. My eyes fell on the fireplace and my escape plan instantly clicked in my head.

"Look at what I have," Abigail said as she dangled a letter from the box I'd left on the chair in front of my face. The front of it was stamped with the logo of a skull and crossbones similar to that seen on a ship.

"Please give that to me," I said, sternly. I glared at her in frustration.

"Not until you tell me more. Orrrrrrrrr I could always burn them," she said, dangling the letter above the flames.

"No. Don't,"

"These are important to you. Why?"

"I have been trusted to keep them safe for Nathaniel

146

Hawthorne,"

"Nate, huh?"

"Yes,"

"I've always despised him," she said, disgusted.

"Why?" I asked.

"Don't ask questions," She clipped, "Who was supposed to be the receiver of these letters?"

"Sophia Katherine Hawthorne," I said, the words tasting salty on my lips. A big lump rose in my throat as Abigail put all the pieces of the puzzle together in her mind and her eyes flashed green for an instant. I thought I imagined it at first, but I knew it had to be real. *What is she going to do next?* Her face went from angry to worried in what seemed like a few seconds and I followed her gaze and saw why. The heavy bootsteps had made their way down the stairs and a blue silhouette of Nathaniel Hawthorne stood at the bottom of the steps. He was completely transparent and wore the exact same outfit he had been wearing only (what I thought) was moments ago before walking the plank. He had the same boots, same three pointed hat, and same overcoat as before. His blue, glowing eyes looked straight into mine and he mouthed two words: *Trap door.*

Abigail stared at him confused as to what he was saying and his ghostly figure turned around and half floated, half walked back up the stairs. I looked down at where he had been standing. There was a square puddle on the floor, where I guessed the floorboards looked slightly different than the rest.

"What did he just say?" Abigail asked.

I shrugged, as if I didn't know either.

The pipes started to creak and moan again as the bathroom sink started to fill up with water. The drain was clogged.

"Oh great!" Abigail said, rushing over to the sink to turn it off.

I rushed towards the trap door, at the bottom of the staircase and looked into the black abyss all the way down the hole. I double checked I had the box in hand as I took one step and fell straight into the black hole.

"Where are you going?" Abigail's fading voice said as I fell, and the door slammed above me.

ASPEN

Chime's Rabbit Cottage, Late Night

As numbers and letters swirled around me with sounds of many different types and intensities, I gradually grew dizzy. The sounds were the cuckoo of a clock, always at nine o'clock. The ding of the clock, always at nine o'clock as well. Or nine bells of a grandfather clock somewhere in the distance. I felt lost within the sounds and sights of time and about to vomit before I was dropped down a wooden hole. I recognized the hole almost immediately and knew exactly where I was going.

When I arrived in the Chime's living room, the image of the sofa, hearth and kitchen seemed to swirl around me.

"I'm going to be sick," I said, and walked swaying back and forth to the sink just before everything came up.

"Sorry about that," Mr. Chimes said, "time traveling is a tricky business,"

"Are you okay, dear?" Mrs. Chimes asked after I was done vomiting.

"Yes?" I squeaked out.

"Follow my finger," Mrs. Chimes said, as she moved it back and forth. My eyes obeyed and followed Mrs. Chime's white finger back and forth. The world seemed to stop spinning for a minute. Just before starting to spin once again, I ran to the sink again. The vomit came up quickly this time.

"My goodness dear. I think you need to lay down," Mrs. Chimes said.

The only word I could utter was, "Yes,"

I rubbed my eyes and followed Mrs. Chimes to our guest room. From the image that seemed to be swinging back and forth now, I saw a lump in both of the other beds. One lump had blonde curls and laid asleep by the window and the other had straight brown hair and rested on the wall to my right. They seemed to be floating.

"Who are the lumps?" I asked, before collapsing on a bed and falling straight asleep.

My sleep was dreamless and long until the sunlight streamed in through the window by the lump I'd seen the night before. I blinked my eyes open and looked around the room to find that the room wasn't spinning anymore. I actually felt much better and sat up in bed.

"Good morning," Fernando said from where he sat on the edge of his bed.

"Morning," I said, stretching.

"William, breakfast time," Fernando said, shaking his shoulder,

"Who's William?" He asked.

"You are," Fernando said.

"Is he okay?" I whispered to Fernando covering my mouth with my right hand.

"Amnesia," He mouthed back to me.

"Ohhhh," I said.

William got out of bed and walked towards the kitchen to get breakfast. Fernando and I fell behind.

"I thought the present day or whenever we are now would fix him," I whispered.

"Apparently not. Maybe the Chimes can help,"

"I hope so. I want him to remember who he is for once. It's exhausting to have to remind him who we are every few minutes,"

"Agreed. Again, as Mr. Chimes said, '"time traveling is a tricky business,"'"

"You never know what might happen," I said.

"I never expected this," Fernando said.

"Me either,"

"Good morning!" Mr. Chimes said, cheerfully.

"What's up?" I asked, giving him a chin up nod.

"You know, the usual," Mr. Chimes said, winking at me.

"What can I get for you all?" Mrs. Chimes asked.

"An omelet and toast?" I asked.

"Coming right up,"

"Pancakes," William said.

"You got it,"

"Waffles," Fernando said.

"They're in the toaster now," Mr. Chimes said.

"Thank you," Fernando said.

After a few more minutes of waiting for our food to cook, we all gathered around the kitchen table and ate our food. William seemed to be extremely tired for the whole meal and kept rubbing his head.

"Let me feel your forehead," Mrs. Chimes said.

William leaned forward.

"You're warm. I can feel your pulse. You really should wrap your head with a bandage," Mrs. Chimes said.

"Can you?"

"Of course. You'd better finish eating first though. No hungry stomachs allowed during healing,"

"Thanks," William said.

"You're welcome. You'll be in my care until you're fully healed," Mrs. Chimes said, smiling sweetly at William.

"In the meantime, we have some things to discuss," Mr. Chimes said, looking at Fernando and me.

"Indeed, we do," I said, taking another bite of food.

"Possibly over tea?" Fernando said, finishing the last bite of his waffles with maple syrup.

"Great idea," Mr. Chimes said, "Let's hop to it,"

I laughed as Mr. Chimes literally hopped towards his tearoom and we followed closely behind. We boiled water in the hot pot and sat down at the center table. Finger food was on the tray in the center of the table, and we picked at it as we waited for the water to boil.

"Today's tea is earl gray," Mr. Chimes said, pouring the hot water into a large teapot to share. We each had a floral teacup at our spots and a floral saucer underneath the teacup.

"Now, enlighten me on your travels through time," Mr. Chimes said.

"We will, but first we have a question for you," I said.

"You see, we were wondering how to get William to remember us and trust us again," Fernando said.

"I think we have to recover the past in order for the present to be going steady," Mr. Chimes said.

"Like fixing the pipes on the boat?" Fernando asked.

"Not necessarily. Think about how Nate felt at the end," Mr. Chimes said.

"He was sad, and didn't want the circumstances to go downhill," Fernando said.

"Exactly. That's his lasting memory, a memory of regret,"

"He regrets not living long enough to marry Sophia Hawthorne," Fernando said, putting the pieces of the puzzle together.

"And what about Sophia Hawthorne?" Mr. Chimes asked me.

"She regrets never sending or even showing her letters to Nate. She wanted it to be a wedding present, so she put it off, not knowing about their lack of time," I added.

"Where do you think Abigail fits in this story?" Mr. Chimes asked.

"Well, she was on the boat when we were prepping it. She used the bathroom and looked extremely guilty when she came out. Ohhhhhh," Fernando said, lighting up. "She's the one who broke the pipe under the sink before the boat even left the port,"

"Do you think she regrets that?" Mr. Chimes asked.

"No. Because she despises Nate Hawthorne. But why does she despise Nate Hawthorne?" Fernando asked.

"That question calls for story time. Let me go grab the book we're reading today," Mr. Chimes said, "Or we could always travel there and see it with our own two eyes,"

"No, thanks," I said, "I think I've had enough time travel for the next few days,"

"What happened?" Fernando asked as Mr. Chimes hopped off to find the book he wanted to read us.

"I got dizzy inside the portal and vomited twice when I came in late last night," I said.

"Oh. I see," Fernando said.

"Fill me in on the part of the story you experienced," I said.

"I will, if you'll tell me your half,"

After we had finished exchanging stories, Mr. Chimes finally returned and poured himself a mug of tea. He had an old, tattered book under his right arm and his spectacles on, ready to read.

"Okay. So, this is actually Abigail's journal from the 1800s. Take a look," Mr. Chimes said.

"Wow. This is cool," I said.

The journal smelled like an old book that had been left in the library for years. A few specks of dust mixed with spider webs rested on the cover. I brushed them off and found the title of the journal: Nabby's Tales.

"How did Abigail get the name Nabby?" I asked.

"'Nabby'" means in this case, rudely inquisitive, meddlesome, sharp-natured, or spiteful. She got the name from building her lifestyle around fitting that name. You'll have to read more into it from her journal,"

I opened the old, tattered journal and was awestruck at the tight cursive that took up the pages.

"This is great penmanship," I said, as I ran my fingers down the ink filled parchment.

"It is indeed," Fernando said, "Read her entries aloud please,"

"*August 1st, 1835. I woke up this morning to the sound of the black cat clawing at my door. How annoying! And here I thought that last night I would somehow be able to sleep in today but instead the cat needed me to feed him. I opened the door, and the black cat ran into my room, hopped onto my bed and I headed downstairs scowling. My sister, Sophia (she goes by Katherine) greeted me in the halls as I walked down the marble staircase to get food for the cat. And that was when I discovered we were out of cat food. So, I put on my best black dress, black hat, and black boots and headed into town to buy food. The* next few words have been scribbled out. I can't read them. Can you?" I

152

asked Fernando.

"No," Fernando said, "Read on,"

"*And as if my day wasn't bad enough already, I literally bumped into Nathaniel Hawthorne (someone whom I deeply liked) at the market. He seemed shocked I'd do such a thing, and I dropped my whole basket of groceries. I feel like such a clutz. He helped me pick them up and when we both stood up together, he took my hand and looked straight into my eyes. His eyes seemed starstruck for a second before he collected himself and I thanked him to which he replied, "It is no problem my dear," I felt like melting at that very moment. And we parted ways.*

Later that day when I arrived home, I fed the cat who wouldn't stop meowing at me and told my sister all about how I liked Nathaniel Hawthorne," I read.

"Wait a minute…… doesn't Sophia marry Nate? Not Abigail?" Fernando asked.

"Yes, that would be correct," Mr. Chimes said.

"Then, I think I know why Abigail despises her sister. Abigail liked Nate at one time, but then Nate got stolen from her by Sophia, and the letters they wrote to each other probably just made Abigail mad,"

"You're exactly right," Mr. Chimes said, "In fact, there's another piece of the story you should see before we continue reading this journal. Follow me to the TV room,"

We followed Mr. Chimes to the TV room, and he dialed up a tape recording on the TV.

"This can play videos too?" I asked.

"Yes. It has many functions,"

Mr. Chimes tinkered with the remote for a little bit longer before clicking enter and a video showed on the screen. On the top read: Ropes Mansion 1841.

The first person to be shown on the screen was Sophia Katherine Hawthorne in tears sitting on the edge of a bed, clutching a pillow to her chest as her chest shook. The top of the screen switched from the location and year to reading: Day negative 1 of wedding day. Someone knocked on the door from off camera.

"Sophia. Can I come in?" Someone asked.

"No," Sophia replied.

"Well too bad, I'm coming in anyway. You need to eat something," Abigail said, dressed in her usual attire: a black dress, black hat, black shoes,

"Okay," Sophia replied.

"Ma said you need to eat this stew and toast,"

"Okay. I don't feel like eating right now. I'll eat it later,"

"Some letters from Nate arrived for you in the mail. I opened them and read every single one. Then guess what I did, Sissy?"

"What?" Sophia asked, her voice shaking slightly.

"I burned them," Abigail said proudly.

"YOU DID WHAT?" Sophia asked.

"Burned the letters," Abigail said triumphantly.

"GO AWAY. NEVER BURN MY MAIL EVER AGAIN," Sophia yelled, as Abigail scurried out the door and down the marble staircase to the sitting room of the mansion. The video cut out just as Sophia started to break down into heart wrenching sobs.

"So, you're telling me that the same skittish, shy Abigail is Sophia's sister, and she burned all the letters?" Fernando said in disbelief.

"I can't believe this," I said.

"Me either," Fernando said.

"What kind of a sister would do such a thing?" I asked.

"Abigail would apparently. She's a wicked, wicked person," Mr. Chimes said, "You'll see what I mean as you read more of her diary,"

"*August 29th, 1840. Ropes Mansion. Today was the day of the ball I've been dying to go to with Nate. So, I went to the dress shop and picked out my best Sunday dress for the ball. I found a pink, fluffy dress I instantly adored. It had long puffy sleeves and a long ruffle skirt. I could only imagine the ways in which the dress would sway back and forth as I danced with Nate tonight. When I got home with the dress my mom eyed me and then the dress and said, "where do you think you're going with that dress, young lady?"*

To which I replied, "To a ball?"

My mom instantly frowned at me as she said, "Didn't you see the

note I left for you at the table?"

"No," I said.

We walked into the kitchen together to find no notes on the table. My eyes proudly went to the crumpled up piece of unread parchment paper that burned in the fireplace. Mom's eyes followed my gaze.

"You burned it. How naughty," Mom said, "You're grounded from the ball tonight. On that piece of parchment paper, I wrote out your list of finishing school late assignments to do. They need to be done whenever you can,"

"How do I know what to do?" I asked.

"I'll rewrite the list. Until I have it rewritten, you are sentenced to your room," Mom said.

I climbed the stairs to my room and instantaneously lit a fire in the fireplace. Both for the warmth and the vibes. I began to undress and redress with layer after layer of the ballgown. Moments after I had managed to wiggle into the rest of my dress, a slip of paper appeared in my room from underneath the crack in the door. I crumpled up that paper as well, not reading a word, and tossing it into the flames.

I needed to make a quick exit to meet Nate at the ball on time, so I did the only thing I could think of: the window.

Downstairs I heard, "Okay. Ma, I'm leaving for the ball,"

"Have fun, Sophia,"

How come she didn't have to do all the chores and missing assignments from finishing school? She's the perfect one. You may never be. Embrace the imperfection.

I heard the carriage pull up to the front side of the house. If you leave now, someone will see you. I waited until the carriage had pulled away from the front of the house to climb out of the window in my long dress and head down the ladder by my window barefoot. Otherwise, I was concerned I would slip and fall. I dropped each shoe one by one from a story up and continued to climb down until I reached the ground.

I slipped my feet into my dress shoes and dashed towards the ball, in an effort not to be late. When I arrived, out of breath and slightly sweaty, I saw Nate waiting outside.

"Just in time my darling. May I?" he said, holding out an arm for me to take.

"Yes, you may," I said, slightly stumbling in my heels.

We walked up the marble stairs together side by side towards the ballroom. The ballroom was decorated like a starry night sky with little lights everywhere. The ceiling had lights projected on it and was dome shaped. The music was classical, rhythmic, and had a story behind it. As I listened, I imagined a game of tag. The music was really fast at first and higher on the keyboard until a lower staccato chord was played and it continued on and on. I saw myself as a kid, playing tag with my friends and derived joy from listening as the memories came back. As time went on, we picked up on the waltz the musician was playing on the piano, so we began our dancing.

1 2 3 4 1 2 3 4. We danced exactly in sync with each other, which made me feel a deep connection to both the beat and Nate. As the musician kept playing, the tempo began to get faster and faster until we were whipping through the steps of the dance rapidly. There was walking back and forth on beats one and two, a twirl on beat three, and a trust fall where I fell into Nate's outstretched arms on beat four, then a repeat. When the musician started to slow down again and hold the final chord, I was out of breath hovering in Nate's arms.

"I'm glad you made it," Nate said.

"I'm glad I got to dance with you," I said, smiling up at him.

"Agreed. I'm going to have a bite to eat," Nate said, walking towards the food table.

I stood in the middle of the ball dance floor watching as the couples danced around me. I felt lost as I watched many couples sway back and forth gazing into each other's eyes. The music had slowed down significantly, and it was almost soothing watching them sway back and forth to the music's beat.

I spotted my sister's teal green dress out of the corner of my eye at the snack table. I turned around and watched as she chatted with Nate. Her smile and slightly rosy cheeks indicated he had said something that made her laugh. He seemed to be enjoying her company as well. His eyes were fixed on hers intensely, as if captivated by her. Sophia waved her fan in front of her face and her perfectly done up hair and seemed to laugh again. Nate offered Sophia her arm and they headed back out onto the dance floor together.

I fumed. I thought Nate was supposed to be my date. I was about to go over to them when I felt my stopwatch buzz against my wrist. Oh great! Ma's going to be checking I did my chores soon. I looked up at the large grandfather clock at the front of the ballroom and it indicated the time was 8:50, not 9pm. I have ten more minutes. As long as I hurry, I'm fine to stay a few more minutes.

The music picked up again and Nate and Sophia went through the same dance moves I had done with him only moments before. I watched and saw the energy between them was very real. When the musician slowed the tempo down once again, my sister crossed her arms over her chest and fell back as Nate caught her with his strong arms. She looked out of breath in Nates' arms from all the rapid dancing. Nate seemed to whisper something in her ear before leaning in for a gentle, tender kiss.

My heart plummeted.

All this time I had thought Nate was mine. My love. My boyfriend. But my sister seemed to steal Nate from me, and I couldn't take the pain and hurt that busted my dreams of getting married to Nate and starting a life together.

A lump rose in my throat as I walked over to Nate to say goodbye and head home before my mother figured out what I'd done. The grandfather clock rang nine times indicating I needed to go. Otherwise, I'd have very stern consequences. I walked over to where Nate and Sophia were swaying back and forth, whispering in each other's ears.

"Nathaniel," I said, trying to keep my voice from shaking.

"Yes," he said, turning towards me.

His ocean blue eyes made me want him all over again, but knowing he was holding my sister at that very moment made me think again. Why does love have to be so complicated? I wish Nate could be mine and my perfect sister didn't have to steal him from me.

"I'm heading home," I said.

"So, soon?" He asked, "We haven't even gotten to the best part of the dance yet. Are you sure you want to go?"

"Yes. Ma's expecting me," I said.

"Didn't you have a chore list to do?" Nate asked.

"No. Late assignments," I snapped.

"I'll see you tomorrow then," Nate said as I curtsied and headed out of the ballroom.

As soon as I was out of the ballroom, I tore both my shoes off and ran all the way towards the mansion. I passed the darkened cemetery with a black iron gate around it, always locked, unless there was a new burial there. I kept running, and the clouds above me began to spit raindrops from the sky. I ran as fast as I could towards the ladder that would lead to my room and climbed up as fast as I could.

When I reached the last rung on the ladder and pulled on the window, it was locked. Oh, great. Ma locked me out again. I climbed back down the ladder, walked around the house through the gardens and looked for the fake brick covering on the right hand side of the trellis. A jasmine vine grew up the trellis, which was very fragrant. The jasmine smelled rich, sweet, and intoxicating with a slight hint of fruitiness.

"Abigail Ropes. What do you think you're doing?" A voice said from behind me as I moved the brick covering away from the trap door, one brick at a time.

"Um,"

"You knew you were grounded, yet you disobeyed my orders to stay in your room tonight and work on your late finishing school assignments," Mom scolded, "How dare you not listen to me,"

I stood there silently.

"You are coming into the house with me, young lady and getting out of that dress and then we'll talk about your consequences," Mom said, angrily.

"Where are my finishing school assignments?" I asked. I knew I had burned them, so Ma had no evidence of the task list or the assignments to show me.

"I'll find them. You're coming in with me NOW," Mom said, grabbing my hand.

By then, the rain had switched from light rain to a full on downpour.

We walked inside, and mom gave me towels to dry off.

"You're off to your room," Mom said, pointing up the stairs

instantly, "NOW,"

I walked up to my room, took off my dress, trying hard not to tear the fabric, and dried off my rain-soaked skin. The rain poured on my window, and I lit a candlestick that sat on the windowsill as I waited for my mom to come in to scold me more. She never came. Instead, I crawled into bed and slept deeply for the next few hours.

"This is a very interesting diary," I said, after finishing the second entry.

"You're very right. It reads more like a narrative than anything," Fernando said.

"Why do you think Abigail decided to show the reality of her circumstances rather than just tell her audience about them?" Mr. Chimes asked.

"She wanted people to feel with her," I said.

"Exactly,"

"I feel so bad for Abigail now that I know her relationship to Sophia Katherine Hawthorne and Nathaniel. They both never got their desired outcome," Fernando said.

"How so?" I asked.

"Nate dies in the *Yorkshire* when it sinks just a few days before his wedding day. Sophia is "widowed" young. Then, we have Abigail who seemed to have loved Nate at a time before Sophia did. Nate gradually faded from Abigail's lifestyle when Sophia came into the picture," Fernando said, "They both never lived to achieve their destiny,"

"Wow. That's sad," I said, humbled by the story we held in our hands.

"You'd better keep reading if you want to know the saddest part," Mr. Chimes said.

"I think I need more tea first," I said.

"Me too," Fernando said.

"Okay. We have strawberry hibiscus tea, earl grey tea, black tea, blueberry tea...,"

"How about strawberry hibiscus?" Fernando suggested.

"Yes, I'd love to try it," I said.

"I'll grab some tissues as well," Mr. Chimes said, "How about I read the next section?"

"Sure," I said, handing Mr. Chimes the journal.

"Aspen, don't you have a similar journal?" Fernando asked.

"Yes," I said, lighting up, "What if...,"

From the expression on Fernandos face I knew exactly what he was thinking, and I was thinking the same thing.

"Before you get your hopes up about this journal, why don't we finish this story first and then we can figure out the journal,"

"Okay," Fernando and I said in unison.

"Read on," I said, as Mr. Chimes sat down in his rabbit sized chair and wiggled a little bit to get comfortable.

"Okay. Here we go," Mr. Chimes said.

"August 30th, 1840: Ropes Mansion. I awoke a few hours later when I heard someone in the house midway through a coughing fit. I crawled out of my bed and followed the sound of the coughing that seemed to echo all the way up and down the halls of the mansion. Eventually, I found the source after I had run down the stairs and into the sitting room. My mom laid on the couch with a bucket by her side coughing up mucus.

"Mom. Mom. Are you okay?" I asked.

She didn't seem to hear me over her loud coughing fit.

"Water," She tried to say in between coughs and mucus spewing out of her mouth into the bucket by the couch.

"I'll be right back," I said, running towards the kitchen.

"Nurse Betty," I called.

"Wait. Pause for a second. They have a family nurse?" Aspen asked.

"Yes. Back in the 1800s it was common if you were royalty to have a family nurse. Mind you, at this day and age, nearly the whole Ropes family had contracted Tuberculous and had been fighting it for a few months," Mr. Chimes explained.

"But not Abigail or Sophia," Fernando confirmed.

"Right," Mr. Chimes said.

"Okay. Continue. Sorry to interrupt," Aspen said.

"Yes Ma'am?" Nurse Betty said.

"Mom needs help," I said, frantically.

Nurse Betty was in the middle of switching out a cooling towel on my father's forehead.

"I'll be there in a minute," Nurse Betty replied.

I filled up a glass of water for my mom and ran back into the family room. Her coughing had stopped, and she lay motionless on the couch.

"Mom. Mom. Wake up," I said, shaking her frantically.

She didn't wake. Nurse Betty rushed into the room and immediately felt my mom's pulse.

"No pulse," she told me as my vision blurred.

Nurse Betty embraced me as I broke down into heart wrenching sobs.

"It'll be okay, dear," She soothed me.

I just continued to sob into her shoulder. Tuberculous was the worst thing that had ever happened to my family. Everyone except me and my sister had some variation of it and their health seemed to be going downhill with each passing day.

"I never said goodbye. She left on an argument," I said, in between sobs.

"What do you mean, dear?" Nurse Betty asked.

"My last memory of her before her coughing fit was her being angry at me for going to the ball against her orders. She was mad and I was naughty. I burned the list of things she wanted me to do and didn't honor her. We never properly said goodbye," I explained in between sobs.

"Betty," My dad called from the kitchen, sounding hoarse.

"Coming," Nurse Betty said.

"It'll be okay darling," Nurse Betty whispered into my ear as I continued to sob, "I need to go help your dad,"

"Okay," I whispered, not trusting my voice to not come out shaky.

"I'll be right back," Nurse Betty promised.

I sat down on the sofa and felt my mom's cold fingers and slid her eyelids closed. It was still dark outside and would be for another few hours until daybreak. I heard movement upstairs and knew it had to be Sophia climbing up to her favorite part of the house. The same place she always went when she needed time to think: The roof.

When Nurse Betty got back, she wore a solemn expression on her face.

"Abigail. Your father has passed," Nurse Betty said, "Tuberculosis. I'm sorry for your loss,"

I ran back up the stairs to my room and cried until I felt like I had no tears left in my eyes and fell into a deep, dreamless slumber.

Mr. Chimes looked up from the entry he was reading and asked, "Should we take a break?"

Fernando wiped the tears from his eyes, and I sat there, my nose running and big salty droplets streaming down my cheeks. *Poor Abigail.*

I nodded.

"Do you have any questions?" Mr. Chimes asked.

"How did Abigail inherit Aspen's Grandma's house?" Fernando asked.

"Actually, due to the time periods, it's the other way around," Mr. Chimes explained.

"So, you're saying that Aspen's Grandma inherited Abigail's house?" Fernando asked.

"Yes,"

"Why did Abigail own that house and what did she keep upstairs?" Fernando asked.

"Great questions, the answers are all in that journal. So, when you're ready we can continue reading," Mr. Chimes said, "But first, read the inside of the cover,"

"Keeper of regrets," Fernando read aloud.

"Read the date too," Mr. Chimes said.

"October 31st. Halloween," Fernando read.

"Now flip to entry four and read it aloud," Mr. Chimes said, "This is less sad than the third,"

"The date is September 14th, 1840. This is the day my dear Aunty Riley passed away. She passed away in her sleep due to Tuberculosis. The days have been passing slowly now, each day full of more grief and morning than the last. I have been living mostly in my bedroom by just the light of the fire as tears stream down my cheeks as I think of the lasting memories of all my family members the day before they passed. I never got to say goodbye to a single one. I was too preoccupied trying to take care of everyone else and trying to find Nurse Betty to help me. Nurse Betty somehow seemed to hold up pretty well in the midst of all this death and mayhem. On the contrary, I have been a huge mess of emotion.

My Uncle Richard passed away just about two days ago due to a coughing fit, similar to that of my mom's. We plan on having a burial ceremony soon yet have been rather preoccupied taking care of everyone else as they have been fighting Tuberculosis. Sophia has been missing from all the chaos over the past couple of days. I'm assuming she's been living on the roof, trying to collect her feelings, and watching the sea for sailboats.

I would do anything just to see my mom or dad one last time to say goodbye to them properly before Tuberculosis took them away. I want them back desperately.

Later this day, the graveyard staff arrived with caskets for my Mother, Father, Uncle, and Aunt and carried them away to a graveyard near the mansion. I watched them as they carried the family members which I loved deeply away to a cemetery I could see from my bedroom window. One of the staff members asked me if I wanted to design their gravestones, and I obliged. I designed a skull and crossbones symbol that would go at the top of the headstone and then their name and dates of birth and death would go beneath that.

The burial ceremony was scheduled for Halloween, just about a month later. I knew the health of my cousin's and other Aunts and Uncles were going downhill as well, so I thought it made the most sense to bury all of them together at the same time. The cemetery was a grassy patch near the mansion with an iron gate around it. I dreaded the day when we would bury my family. It only meant one thing: they were really gone and like a stone, I carried the guilt of never properly *saying goodbye to any family members before they passed.*

"Okay. So, I think we know the meaning of the Keeper of Regrets now," Fernando said.

"Yes, but there's more to it," Mr. Chimes said, flipping over a few entries, "Here's the entry from Burial Day on Halloween. Is this story starting to sound at least a little bit familiar?"

"A little bit. There are some parts that sound like something I've lived through but others that don't quite fit yet," I said.

"Like what?" Mr. Chimes asked.

"The cemetery outside the Rope's mansion. I know exactly where that is,"

"And?"

"I've never been able to get inside that cemetery. It's always locked to tourists and locals. There isn't anywhere you can buy tickets for a tour of the cemetery either. No one seems to have the keys," I said.

"Right. Now, read the burial day entry and you'll see why,"

"The date is October 31st. All Hallows Eve. The year is 1841. Sophia and I are the only people still living in the Ropes Mansion. And the mansion is the quietest it's been in a long time. There aren't the sounds of people coughing mucus out of their lungs from Tuberculosis or the rushed footsteps of Nurse Betty running up and down the stairs or in and out of the kitchen. Instead, it's utterly, eerily quiet. I haven't slept in days and the skin under my eyes is purple.

I've been too busy writing up my funeral speeches for each and every family member I've lived with since I was born in this mansion. It's taken far too long. Sometimes I get frustrated when I start writing something and it sounds good one minute and sounds awful the next. So, to express my disappointment, I scream into a pillow. Then, I try again, and again and again. I have a mountain of crumpled parchment paper on the right side of my desk. I stare at the pile of messed up attempts until I can't seem to keep my eyes open anymore and fall asleep with my head on the desk.

I awoke moments later when Sophia is gently nudging my arm to wake me.

"Hey. We need to go to the burial," Sophia said gently.

"Okay," I said, getting up from the desk, feeling raw, tired and angry.

I opened my wardrobe and frowned when I saw the pink dress I had worn to the ball with Nate, which overall turned out to be a bad idea. Every time I've looked at that dress since the night of the ball, I've just been reminded of a person whom I've fallen for and never been able to love fully. I pulled on a black dress, black boots, and a black pointy hat. I straightened my hair and headed out into the streets of Salem Massachusetts with Sophia by my side.

"Where have you been over the past few days?" I asked Sophia.

"The roof, watching for my sailor to return someday,"

"He won't," I said.

"Why?"

"The Yorkshire sank due to a broken pipe,"

"Oh,"

"The burial for the sailors is this Sunday," I said.

"Okay,"

As we walked, the bell calling everyone to the cemetery rang nine times. The bells were slow, distant and solemn. I stood at the front of the cemetery with the rest of the crowd as we listened to the last few vibrations of the last bell. Then, we started to sing the hymn we always sang at burials: Leaning on Everlasting arms.

Then, the Minister, William Ropes opened the ceremony in prayer.

"In the name of the Father, the Son, and the Holy Spirit. The opening verse is from the book of Psalms, 'In peace I will lie down and fall asleep for you alone Lord make me feel secure.'"

Minister Ropes took a key out of his right pocket and unlocked the gate to the cemetery where the bodies rested in caskets. The three altar servers behind the minister blessed each casket with incense that smelled of frankincense.

"We would like to request that all of you stay outside the cemetery gate as there are many holes in the ground where we're going to put the caskets," Minister William explained.

The smoke from the incense wafted up towards the sky. I

imagined all their souls floating up with the incense, yet I knew somewhere deep inside that they all somehow had something they regretted, that weighed them down like rocks until they no longer carried their regrets. They all had business on this earth that had been left undone.

Minister William prayed over each soul and blessed them all. From the tender way in which he acted I could tell he fully believed in the power of divine prayer. He knew there was something far greater than him that called him here today. I was only half listening as I looked around the cemetery. There was an oak tree at the upper right of the cemetery that shaded a small collection of headstones with a few holes in the ground nearby it. The headstones were spread all around the cemetery, each with a skull and crossbones on it.

When Minister William asked if I had any funeral speeches, I politely said "no". And he continued on with his message today. He talked about how we all needed to trust in the Lord in order to dwell in safety. Without trust, we would have nobody to lean on or confide in. "As human beings our job is to make every second count, because you never know what might happen.

"Always live for the present moment and live life to the fullest. I think all nine of these souls here today have lived their lives to the fullest, and we are here to celebrate their lives," He said before closing with a sign of the cross and a blessing.

Minister Williams closed the gate once again as he processed out of the cemetery and locked it once again. This time, I noticed the handle of the key was shaped like a clock. The hour hand pointed to nine and the minute hand pointed towards twelve. It indicated the time of the funeral ceremony and the number of bells that were rung: one for each soul we buried today.

We eventually sang the closing hymn quietly, solemnly, until we all headed out of the cemetery area and back to the mansion.

"I'm going on a walk around town," Sophia said.

"Okay,"

I walked back to the mansion and headed upstairs to light a fire in the fireplace. I needed to burn my missed attempts at a funeral speech. I felt like I had been so clueless when it came to writing wedding speeches. I dropped page after page into the amber flames, and while I was burning things, I decided to destroy the evidence that I had been to the ball on that cold, rainy evening with Nate. I pulled the pink ball gown out of my wardrobe and tossed it into the flames. It caught fast. I stood maybe a few inches from the flames.

ASPEN

"Is that the last entry?" I asked.

"Yes and no," Mr. Chimes said.

"Yes, as in it shows the end of Abigails earthly life. No as in she continues to live on in her ghostly life,"

"But there are no entries as she lives in her ghostly life, right?"

"Yes,"

"Why did she stop writing?" I asked.

"Because ghosts only focus on their undone business and not anything else,"

"Okay, so their purpose is to complete whatever is lingering and be freed from earth," Fernando said.

"Yes,"

"Honey, we have a bit of a predicament...," Mrs. Chimes called from the kitchen.

"I'm coming darling," Mr. Chimes called back.

To us, he said, "Think about what you just said. It's important,"

He hopped down the hallway and Fernando and I watched from where we stood in the tearoom. The door to the bedroom William was sleeping in was left ajar. Mr. Chimes' jaw dropped as he saw what happened. Fernando and I rushed over to him and looked at the room. There was a glowing purple circle right next to William's bed and William was gone.

WILLIAM'S POV

Aspen's Grandmas house

"Who are you?" Someone asked me as the world came into focus.

"Huh?" I asked, confused and disoriented.

"Tell me who you are. I know you know deep down," This voice was a woman's voice that sounded vaguely familiar.

I was silent. I thought as hard as I could yet came up with nothing.

"Let me make you a beverage that might help you remember,"

"I'm hungry," I said as my stomach grumbled.

"I'll make you a drink and a bowl of mac n cheese," The woman's voice said again.

The voice was starting to sound very familiar. I couldn't find a place where it sounded familiar from. I tried to open my eyes, and it was painful. It felt as though they were swollen shut. I opened them a sliver.

"Remember how Mac n Cheese used to be your favorite meal when you were little?"

I thought for a moment, and tiny flashes of memories came back to me. I was at my grandma's house. The scent of pumpkin spice wafted in the air and I couldn't help but think about a large, sweet, delicious pumpkin pie.

My grandma had her back turned to me and worked at the stove to make the Mac n Cheese just right. When she turned around with the comforting bowl of steaming bowl of hot Mac n Cheese, I saw that she wore a golden chain around her neck with a key at the end of it. It shimmered against the light of the kitchen, and I took a bite of mac n cheese savoring the flavor.

Hot Chocolate with Memory Mallows

Ingredients:
One packet hot cocoa powder
One cup water
One package mini marshmallows
A pinch of cinnamon sugar
A pinch of memory peppermint

Memory Mac N Cheese

Ingredients:
1 lb. dried elbow pasta
1/2 cup unsalted butter
1/2 cup all purpose flour
1 1/2 cups whole milk
2 1/2 cups half and half **see chef tips #1 below**
4 cups shredded medium cheddar cheese divided
(measured after shredding)
2 cups shredded Gruyere cheese divided
(measured after shredding)
1/2 Tbsp. salt
1/2 tsp. black pepper
1/4 tsp. paprika smoked paprika is our favorite!

Instructions:
1. Preheat oven to 325 degrees F and grease a 3 qt baking dish (9x13"). Set aside.
2. Bring a large pot of salted water to a boil. When boiling, add dried pasta and cook 1 minute less than

the package directs for al dente. Drain and drizzle with a little bit of olive oil to keep from sticking.

3. While water is coming up to a boil, shred cheeses and toss together to mix, then divide into three piles. Approximately 3 cups for the sauce, 1 1/2 cups for the inner layer, and 1 1/2 cups for the topping.

4. Melt butter in a large saucepan over MED heat. Sprinkle in flour and whisk to combine. Mixture will look like very wet sand. Cook for approximately 1 minute, whisking often. Slowly pour in about 2 cups or so of the half and half, while whisking constantly, until smooth. Slowly pour in the remaining half and half plus the whole milk, while whisking constantly, until combined and smooth.

5. Continue to heat over MED heat, whisking very often, until thickened to a very thick consistency. It should almost be the consistency of a semi thinned out condensed soup.

6. Remove from the heat and stir in spices and 1 1/2 cups of the cheeses, stirring to melt and combine. Stir in another 1 1/2 cups of cheese, and stir until completely melted and smooth.

7. In a large mixing bowl, combine drained pasta with cheese sauce, stirring to combine fully. Pour half of the pasta mixture into the prepared baking dish. Top with 1 1/2 cups of shredded cheeses, then top that with the remaining pasta mixture.

8. Sprinkle the top with the last 1 1/2 cups of cheese and bake for 15 minutes, until cheesy is bubbly and lightly golden brown.

"Why am I here?" I asked.

"Trust what you know deep down inside. Trust your heart. Trust your intuition and you will find out why you're here," The older woman said.

I couldn't stop staring at the golden chain around her neck with the key attached to it. I took another bite of Mac n cheese, and a flash of memory came back to me. A younger version of a girl who looked familiar but couldn't remember the name of was playing with me.

"It turns out your dreams are not what they seem," the older woman said.

Another flash of a memory came back to me. This time the same girl from before and I were sitting next to the old lady that stood before me while she read us a bedtime story. With another whoosh of air, I was back in the old lady's kitchen taking another bite of Mac N Cheese.

"Why don't you have some hot cocoa with Marshmallows and head upstairs to bed?" The older lady said, as she gave me a cozy cup of hot cocoa.

I knew she was right, but something in me prompted me to stay and ask something that had been on my mind for a while.

"Can I please have the key you're wearing?"

"Why yes, my darling. Know one thing, this key holds memories as it has been passed down through many generations. It's yours now, William, now go unlock who you truly are," The old lady said as she gave me the key necklace. I held it in my hand for a moment and felt the chill of the key and the weight as it sat in my outstretched hand. It shone in the light.

William. William. William. I thought to myself as I my feet carried me up the stairs and to a hallway with many closed doors full of darkness. Each door had the same shade golden lock that matched the key. *Is William really my name?*

I unlocked the first door in the hallway with the key the older woman had given me and took one step before starting to fall through time and space.

When I finally stopped falling, I found myself sitting by a hospital bed in the 1800's. I was dressed in black from head to toe and wore a black cross necklace. I held a rosary in my right hand as I stared into my mother's eyes. She had burn scars on her hands, and all the way up her left arm. She wore an oxygen mask, and I watched her. My eyes teared up as I watched her.

"Mom. I love you so much," I whispered into the air around us.

She was in a coma state, unaware of her surroundings, somewhere in the abyss of nothingness.

"I want you to come back. I miss you," I said, as warm wet droplets ran down my cheeks and onto my mother.

"I'll pray over you now. In peace you will lie down now as the Lord makes you feel secure. He will rescue you from the fire, and the burns by extinguishing it with water,"

When I said water, rain began to fall from the heavens as if the Lord had heard and answered my prayer at the same time.

"William. I'm here with you, my son," My mother whispered into the space between us.

The warmth I felt in my heart made my face light up in joy, and relief. That was when I noticed the gold chain with a key on it that sat on my mom's beside table.

"I love you, my William, with all my heart. Trust your heart by taking the key with you to remember me by,"

"Thank you,"

And my dearly beloved mother became very still.

WILLIAM

Christmas, Stardust Story

I was walking through the hallway again and unlocked the second door on the left. Before stepping through it and falling through space and time all over again. This time, the air was cold on my skin as I fell and fell. Snow began to fall with me and silver bells played in the distance.

"Grandma," Aspen said, running up to our grandmother and giving her a big hug. Her parents, Aunt Anna and Uncle Daniel Ropes followed quickly behind.

"Hi William," Aspen said, giving me a hug.

"Hi Fernando," Aspen said, hugging him as well.

"You're all my favorite cousins ever," Aspen said as we all ran towards the family room to play games together until dinner. Our parents chatted, laughed and then we all sat down together at the table to enjoy a wonderful meal together.

"Can we do a story tonight, grandma?" Aspen asked excitedly.

"Of course. But first, in order to tell the story, I need some props. Let's start after dinner," Grandma said.

After we had all gathered in the living room for a bedtime story our grandmother began.

"William, darling. Have you been aware of the spice cabinet I keep in my kitchen this whole time with glittery dust of many different colors?"

"Yes,"

"Have you ever wondered how it's made?"

"Yes,"

"It's made from all the stars in the galaxy, and it's been passed down from generation to generation in our family to deliver prosperous dreams from our ancestors. Each time you've dreamed, it's been with the use of the stardust I keep in that cabinet. Every dream has a purpose: to show you more about yourself than you knew before. Let me ask you this one question and you don't have to answer aloud – who are you really?"

"Each color of stardust indicates the intensity of the dream and if they're bad or good. If I use red stardust, then you will have a fire-related dream. If I use blue stardust, there will be snow or water in your dream. The list goes on. The more you use the longer it lasts. Since you have proven yourself worthy, William, I hereby pass the cottage and the stardust onto you. You have discovered who you are, William Minister,"

"Thank you,"

"May the power of our ancestors be with you always and may you always use it for good, not evil,"

"Aspen, you've already found this book in your bedroom at home and used it to communicate with me from time to time. I want you to keep it in your possession for years to come. This book contains the history of all our ancestors from the very beginning of creation. All you must do is ask,"

"Thank you,"

The clock grandma handed to Fernando wasn't just any clock. It had numbers written in cursive and a different tree leaf every multiple of three. Where 3 should have been was an oak leaf. Where 6 should have been there was a maple leaf, and where 9 should have been there was a pine leaf. In the center of the clock was a tree, connecting all the types of leaves together. On the back of the clock, there was an engraving that read, "Trees wobble, may your roots always stay strong,"

"Fernando, I have a clock for you. This clock isn't just any clock though. Since you lost your mom, I thought your mom could live on within time. So, any time you want to see your mom again, in dreams or in memory, all you have to do is crank the clock to nine or the oak leaf and you'll see your mom right there. She will live on within both of you, William and Fernando,"

"Thank you, Grandma," Fernando and I said.

That was when my eyes caught on something outside the window – a graveyard.

Aspen following my gaze asked, "Grandma, why do you have a graveyard outside your house?"

"That was from my grandma, Abigail, keeper of regrets. She owned this house before my time,"

FERNANDO'S POV
Chime's Cottage

"Mr. Chimes, where are we going?" Fernando asked.

"You'll see,"

And we spiraled down, down, down, until we reached Grandma's house.

The ghost of Abigail lingered in the kitchen. It was dark.

"In this time, this house belongs to Abigail," Mr. Chimes whispered to me.

"Abigail," Mr. Chimes said.

"WHAT?" she asked, swooping towards us.

Mr. Chimes held his hands up and walked backwards. I did the same.

"We want to help," Mr. Chimes said, "After all I'm the master of time,"

"And HOW could you do that?" she asked, crossing her ghostly transparent arms.

"I could give you a potion, so you can go back and say goodbye to your ancestors. Not in a dream or memory – for real," Mr. Chimes said.

I looked deep into Abigails eyes and saw sorrow, grief, and longing deep inside her.

"Please," She said, "It is what I regret most. Not saying goodbye properly to my family. I loved them deeply. I wish I would have been a better child too and honored my parents more,"

"You can do that if you're willing to give us the love letters between Nate and Katherine,"

"Anything to see my family again," The ghost of Abigail said, tears streaming down her ghostly face.

Abigail conjured up the love letters as if they were brand new.

"I will deliver these to the rightful owner and free Nate and Katherine's spirits as well. Thank you, Abigail,"

Mr. Chimes gave her the potion.

"Thank you, master of time," She said.

And her spirit was freed forever. All the souls in the graveyard outside Grandmas house floated up to the heavens and it felt as though the world sighed in relief.

Present day: Aspen's house. Family gathering of Ropes and Lowell's. (Fernando's Pov)

"Hi. Welcome home," Aspen said, opening the door as her parents walked into the house, which had been nicely cleaned for this occasion.

"How was your two weeks of independence?" Mrs. Ropes asked.

"Great. We had lots of adventures," Aspen said.

"I'm glad,"

"So, how was your cruise?" William asked.

"Crazy. I'm so glad the plumbers arrived when they did, otherwise, I don't think we would have been able to make it home. Turns out, there was only a minor leak that just needed a little patch, which was causing a major malfunction. Pretty crazy, isn't it?" Mr. Ropes said.

"Yes,"

Knock. Knock.

Aspen opened the door, and my father was on the other side.

"Dad. I'm so glad you made it home. They finally freed you from the Salem Inn!" I said, giving him a big hug. William followed my lead.

"How did they free you?" William asked.

"Turns out, Nate and Katherine went back to live out the rest of their lives and their relationship. Their letters were delivered to the rightful owner. This meant that no more ghosts, at least that I know of, haunt the Salem Inn anymore,"

The conversation and food that night was lively and fulfilling. It lifted everyone's spirits, to all be together around a crowded table sharing stories of the past two weeks, or what seemed like two weeks.

30 YEARS LATER

"Come on, kiddos. Let's go trick or treating with Uncle Fernando and Uncle William," Aspen said, prompting her kids to follow her. The twin girls, Ava and Shelby came out wearing matching pink sport suits with pink bags to put their candy in.

"You too look adorable," Aspen said.

"We did great, didn't we sis?" Ava said.

"We are twinning," Shelby replied, and they did their favorite secret handshake by high fiving and fist bumping. Then they turned around to high five down low and turned back around to face each other to high five up high once again.

Uncle William held a little boy's hand.

"Hi Everett," Shelby said, smiling.

Everett wore a superman costume and matched his twin brother, Ethan, wearing a similar superman costume.

"I need to get a picture of all of you guys before you go off trick or treating," Aspen said.

"Smile,"

Aspen snapped a picture on her phone of all the kids, with their arms around each other smiling brightly.

"Okay. Stay within my line of sight and have fun trick or treating," Aspen said.

And the kids were off on a windy evening as the sun began to set, the sky became darker, and darker. There was an eerie feeling lingering in the air.

THE FOLLOWING RECIPIES ARE AVAILABLE AT:

Chocolate Cake: https://sallysbakingaddiction.com/triple-chocolate-layer-cake/

Cornbread Muffins: https://www.lecremedelacrumb.com/best-moist-cornbread-muffins/

Mac n' Cheese: https://www.thechunkychef.com/family-favorite-baked-mac-and-cheese/#wprm-recipe-container-9151

Sweet Potato Stew: https://www.themediterraneandish.com/vegetarian-sweet-potato-stew/#tasty-recipes-32868-jump-target

Trust Me Tart: https://www.simplyrecipes.com/recipes/berry_tart/

ABOUT THE AUTHOR

Aubrey Kubiak recently graduated from Colgan High School. She was in the CFPA Colgan Creative Writing Program. After graudation, she plans to go to West Virginia University in Morgantown, West Virginia and major in Agribusiness and Applied Economics with a Minor in Food Science. In her spare time, Aubrey likes to hike, run, travel, read and write.